# A CANDLE IN A CATHEDRAL

---

## A BRAD WALKER SUSPENSE NOVEL

### DALE LOVIN

ILLUMIFY
MEDIA.COM

# A CANDLE IN A CATHEDRAL

*A Brad Walker Suspense Novel*

## DALE LOVIN

ILLUMIFY
MEDIA.COM

Published by
Illumify Media Global
www.IllumifyMedia.com
*"Let's bring your book to life!"*

Paperback ISBN: 978-1-959099-31-4

Typeset by Jennifer Clark
Cover design by Debbie Lewis

*Printed in the United States of America*

*Within our world and across our nation, there exist many forgotten people. Because of race, gender, societal perceptions, or misguided history, many people are overlooked or forgotten. Perhaps none are more often or more negligently failed than victims. Crime, hatred, neglect, ignorance, poverty—all deliver victims. And, as told in the pages of this story, not all victims are human.*

*A Candle in a Cathedral is dedicated to those who fight for victims. Every day, law enforcement, the legal profession, first responders, educators, mental health providers, and ordinary citizens intercede on behalf of victims. Without these heroes, our world would be a dark place.*

# PROLOGUE

What is man without the beasts?
If all the beasts were gone,
men would die from great loneliness of spirit,
for whatever happens to the beasts also happens to man.
All things are connected.
Whatever befalls the earth befalls the children of the earth.

*Chief Seattle*
*Suquamish and Duwamish tribes*

A cathedral … a place between heaven and earth.

*Anselm Kiefer*

## ONE

He loved the night. But it was more than just the night. Pungent odors of rotting leaves in damp soil, together with the pre-dawn chill of early September, made him feel alive like nothing else. A sliver of moon dangled at treetop level. With the luster of a polished pearl, its luminescence cast a soft glow over a silent forest. Seated on the ground, his back against a tree with a crossbow comfortably resting in his lap, the man inhaled a deep breath, closed his eyes and waited.

Seconds became minutes. The moon sank and the blush of dawn made a gradual arc across the sky. A breeze stirred. Pine trees seemed to breathe morning's air while aspen leaves fluttered like weightless fairies. The man shifted his weight. With the crossbow now firmly in his hands, his shoulders hunched as he leaned forward. More minutes passed. The sky became a rose-tinted canvas. A clearing that had been obscured within darkness gradually came into view. Standing water of an oozing spring created an oasis of lush grass. Water droplets glistened as they captured the sun's first light.

Moving with the grace of a ballerina, a doe stepped into the clearing. Head held high and ears erect, she gingerly lifted one leg at a time in a cautious advance toward water. With instinctive confidence in Mother's wisdom, her fawn followed. Even in diminutive light, the young creature's eyes glowed with the wonderment of a new day.

Two more does appeared. The fawn turned her head in greeting and, in a prancing gait, trotted to join the newcomers. Coming together at the spring, the adults scanned their surroundings. Searching for sights, sounds or smells of danger, their ears twitched and nostrils flared. After cautious moments, they lowered their heads to drink.

A buck approached, his antlers shimmering as a crown upon a muscled body. Holding his head perfectly erect, he stood motionless in silent vigilance while the does and fawn drank.

With a scarcely perceptible hiss, an arrow's shaft sliced the air. In the time of a blink, three surgically sharpened stainless-steel blades impaled the buck's upper body. Muscle, heart, and lungs shredded as the blades lacerated the life-giving cavity. As his heart exploded, the wounded animal leapt into the air, and in a seizure of confusion and terror, staggered toward protection of the forest.

Speaking a command into a two-way radio as he stood up, the man jogged toward the place where his arrow had found its target. The scientifically designed arrow tip had performed as intended. Configured to cause maximum bleeding, splotches of blood were easily tracked. Within feet of entering the canopy of the forest, the man saw the collapsed body of the buck. Gasping in the final moments of life, a gurgle escaped from the deer's throat.

Unable to move, the buck watched as a towering figure approached. The brown globe of the doomed animal's eyes swelled in uncomprehending fear. With gruesome efficiency, the blade of a game saw made its first slice. Beginning above the shoulders, hide ripped and muscle sheared. The spinal cord severed.

Crossbow in one hand and bloodied trophy in the other, the man jogged to a dirt road where a pickup truck waited. The man behind the wheel, seeing his companion approach while holding the buck's head, smiled and extended a thumbs-up gesture.

# TWO

A MUG GRASPED SNUGLY within his palms and both arms resting on the porch railing, Brad Walker welcomed the ascending spiral of steam warming his face. Hunching his shoulders, he inhaled, savoring the aroma of coffee at dawn. This was his favored time. The light of a newborn day with crisp mountain air were treasured moments. The village of Red River, New Mexico, seemed to exhale a peaceful yawn as hues of pink colored towering peaks of the Sangre de Cristo Mountains.

"Whatcha doin' out here all by yourself? You think some rich and beautiful woman will somehow materialize and sweep you away to be her sex slave?" Brad felt the warmth of Juanita Ferris press against his body as she extended the blanket she had wrapped about her shoulders. Standing straight, Brad accepted her offer and smiled as she worked to cover them both within her favorite wrap, a Navajo weave of soft wool.

Her head tilted, Juanita gazed up to Brad before speaking. "I'm not sure which I need first, a morning kiss or a sip of that coffee you are holding."

"Not your choice, young lady." Kissing her expectant lips before passing the coffee mug, Brad smiled. "Sip away, my dear, sip away. Anything to keep you from becoming a grouch."

Giving a hip bump as she lifted the mug, Juanita was silent for a moment before exhaling a soft sigh of contentment. "Mornings like this make me think maybe we should move here. You know I'm struggling. I truly am tired of the courtroom, criminals, trials and the whole lawyer rat race in Albuquerque. We could come here, buy ourselves a cozy little place and live happily ever after."

With a muffled grunt, Brad reached for the coffee mug. "Yeah, I hear your talk about being burned out in the lawyer world. I may be wrong, but my money says you would make it maybe a month before you started to go crazy. You couldn't live without prosecuting cases and the buzz you get with every trial. You would go nuts and then you sure as heck would drive me nuts." Brad lifted the mug to his lips and concluded. "That's the way I see it, anyway."

"Well, since you've walked away from all those years you spent as an FBI agent and no longer do anything productive with your life, you only get half a vote. That makes me the boss. I'll be the one to make this decision." Juanita pressed her body closer to Brad as he placed an arm about her shoulder. Moments passed in silence as they shared coffee and basked in the serenity of morning's quiet.

Juanita broke the moment. "I'm not sure if I'm just dreaming or if I'm actually making plans. But come on, Brad, it does sound idyllic, don't you think? Just look at Uncle Foster. He runs this gift shop, meets all kinds of different people, makes a little money and enjoys life. When it's not summer or winter tourist season, he's off to who knows where for tons of vacation days. I've thoroughly enjoyed the past week here, giving him a hand while his wife and regular help took some time off. This has been a great way to spend a bit of my vacation. Plus, I've learned a lot about Native American pottery and jewelry, both of which I love. I could get used to this. And you," she continued with sarcasm now in her voice, "have certainly enjoyed more fishing time than you've ever had." Juanita gave another hip bump. "While I'm here slaving away in Uncle Foster's gift shop, you are off to the family ranch listening to Uncle Ernie spin his tall tales and lies. Then you go fishing on that beautiful stream that runs through his land."

Juanita laughed softly and shook her head. "Those old coots are a pair. It is rare indeed to find brothers who are as close as those two. Uncle Ernie and Uncle Foster grew up side by side. The only things they knew were castrating cattle, shoveling manure and repairing tractors or trucks that were always broken down. No one could believe it when Uncle Foster left the ranch to go to college. They darned sure couldn't believe it when he came back home sporting a wife from the big city and announcing they would be opening a gift shop."

"Yep, I gotta give it to you. They are a pair. And you are correct, this has been quite a vacation for me." Leaning over the railing, Brad drained the remaining few drops of coffee from the mug on to the ground. "I agree with you about the idyllic nature of this area. I love it here. And the lifestyle your Uncle Foster seems to have, how could I argue?" With a shake of his head, Brad's voice lowered. "But something about this morning has not been idyllic at all for me. I can't explain it, Juanita, but something is not feeling right. The strangest voice is whispering inside my head. Or hell, maybe it's my gut. But something is telling me that something about this morning is haywire. Somewhere, somehow, things aren't right."

Turning her head, Juanita looked intently at Brad but remained silent.

Looking straight ahead, Brad thought before again speaking. "I was awakened well before daylight this morning. It was very unusual, but an owl was right outside our window. He kept hooting every few seconds." With a grin, Brad looked at Juanita. "By the way you were snoring, I assumed you weren't hearing a thing."

"I don't snore, smart ass, so don't even try going there."

"Oh, okay. I guess it must have been a helicopter hovering over the rooftop. But judging from the way that owl was conducting his serenade, it just seemed like he was trying to get my attention, like he wanted to tell me something. That's when I felt the sensation that something was wrong. As his hooting antics went on and on, a bad feeling really began to gnaw at me. I had no idea what it might be.

So, I got up and tiptoed from our room and down the stairs to the gift shop. I looked around and everything was exactly as it should be. I sat down behind the counter and just listened to the silence for a bit. I reminisced for a while about the time we've had here in your uncle's shop and how nice it has been to have the little bedroom and kitchen all to ourselves. When it's time to open for business, your Uncle Foster shows up with a big smile and takes over. You are simply his helper. No pressures at all and you have had a ton of fun greeting customers and meeting some interesting people."

Juanita nodded. "I have truly loved every day."

"But my sense of unease didn't go away, in fact it got worse. I decided to make coffee and then came outside thinking morning air and dawn would take care of everything. No such luck. As soon as I stepped outside, the rude-ass owl that had awakened me flew right in front of my face and disappeared. It was like he had finished bothering me and it was time to leave. But the bad feelings I was experiencing didn't fly away with him. Now, after quite a bit of time, I still have a sense that something rotten is in the air. I feel like the sun is too heavy, struggling to even rise up in the sky." Brad took a breath. "I hate to say this, but stuff like this has happened before. I feel an omen, Juanita. I feel an omen of something bad. How to explain beyond that, I have no idea."

Reaching to grasp Brad's hand, Juanita gave a hard squeeze before speaking. "Listen to me, babe. The fact that you listened to your intuition in the past is the very reason you and I are sharing this life. We've talked countless times about the crazy and inexplicable visions, dreams, or whatever they were, something from another world, that somehow brought us together." Juanita pressed Brad's hand again. "I love you, Brad Walker. I can't offer any explanation for how we found each other but I know enough to listen when your senses sound an alarm for some sort of omen."

Looking up to the sky, Juanita was thoughtful for a moment. "Uncle Foster doesn't need my help in the shop until this afternoon. So, how about we take a drive out to the ranch and see Uncle Ernie and Aunt Flo. We can laugh at their hilarious antics for a while.

That's always good for us both. And who knows, maybe it will help clarify your thoughts."

Facing Juanita, Brad studied her eyes for several moments before again kissing her. This time the kiss lingered. "I love you too, Miss Juanita. And by the way, you taste much better than that lousy coffee I brewed. Let's go inside. Sneak back to that little bedroom that I left way too early this morning. We need to start this day off properly. After that, a drive to see your crazy aunt and uncle sounds perfect."

# THREE

Mid-morning sun gave warning of afternoon heat, thunderstorms or maybe both. Following northern New Mexico's highway known as the Enchanted Circle, Juanita and Brad ascended Bobcat Pass before spiraling down toward the village of Eagle Nest. The upper reaches of Moreno Valley opened into rolling hills of ranch land and Juanita hummed along with the radio. The vigilant gaze of Wheeler Peak, New Mexico's highest point, accompanied them, feeling like a close friend. Leaving the highway for a dirt road, they lowered the windows of Brad's truck while traversing bumps and ruts in silence. Upon cresting a hill that offered a view of the ranch house and outbuildings, treasured memories of childhood visits brought a smile to Juanita's face.

As Brad pulled his truck between the house and barn, Juanita broke into full laughter. "Oh my, this is going to be classic." Juanita pointed to a dilapidated pickup truck with an even more dilapidated trailer attached. The coveralls-clad figure of her Uncle Ernie was bent beneath the opened hood of the pickup truck while her Aunt Flo stood beside her husband. Hands on hips, shaking her head and obviously speaking with exasperation, Flo's animation clearly signaled a disagreement.

"This is what movies are made of." Juanita spoke with pure joy as she opened the truck door and stepped out. "Come on over for a ring-side seat."

Having heard the approach of Brad's truck and the slamming of its doors, Aunt Flo looked up. Lifting a hand to wave before cupping her hands about her mouth, she shouted a warning. "Better stand back, kids, something over here is gonna blow any second. And let me tell you, it will not be pretty." Rolling her eyes, Flo stooped to place her head beneath the opened hood. With her face only inches from her husband, she shouted with a voice loud enough to be heard for miles. "Ernie, we have company. Come up for air and try to behave yourself."

Juanita and Brad slowly approached the pickup truck and trailer as they watched Ernie's torso retreat from under the hood. A groan and a curse drifted from his mouth as he cautiously straightened his back and twisted back and forth. "My wife is a pain in my butt and arthritis is a pain in my back. Not sure which I need to get rid of first." Ernie grinned. "At the moment, I'm leaning toward the wife, but I'll hold off on a final decision for just a bit." Wiping his hands on a rag smeared with crusted dirt and ancient oil stains, Ernie extended open arms to Juanita for a hug. "How's my spectacularly gorgeous niece?" He paused. "And not to mention the best damned lawyer in the state of New Mexico."

Ignoring Ernie's dirty hands and clothing, Juanita flung her arms about her uncle with an embrace of love. "Hello Uncle Ernie. I see Aunt Flo is giving you a lesson in auto mechanics. How's it going? You learning anything?" Juanita broke her embrace and turned to hug her aunt. Her eyes dancing, Juanita asked with mock sincerity, "Is there any hope for this guy or should you just give up? Try teaching him something else? Maybe violin lessons or yoga classes?"

Brad remained by the trailer, enjoying the exchange between people who obviously cared deeply for one another. He had to smile as he observed the contents of Ernie's trailer: a half portion of a hay bale, empty oil cans, scattered tools, post hole diggers, rusted horseshoes and a bucket with more holes than swiss cheese. Across the top of the conglomeration lay a chainsaw that appeared to be relatively new and in working order. Easily spotted in the mix were empty beer cans and discarded wrappers that betrayed a love for Snickers.

"So, little girl, you continue to let this old has-been FBI guy hang around you?" Ernie extended his hand to Brad as he continued speaking to Juanita. "Give me a week and I could probably make a rancher out of him."

Before Brad could reply, Flo interjected with authority. "If Brad here becomes a rancher, that would sure as heck give us one more than we have right now! Plus, my money says he's already a better mechanic." Flo interrupted her husband's handshake to throw her arms about Brad. "So glad you are here and pay no attention to my husband. As usual, he is confused and constipated. So just smile and shake your head. Up and down or side to side, one way or another. He'll never know the difference."

Throwing his hands into the air Brad laughed and exclaimed, "I'm not very smart but I darned sure know enough not to get between the two of you. What's the problem with your truck, Ernie?"

"Well, everything works just fine when the sun shines, birds sing, and butterflies fly. But on the rare occasions when it does rain around here, of course it absolutely pours. And that's when the danged window wipers go dead as George Washington." Ernie pointed to something unseen under the hood. "But as soon as the rain stops, the damned wipers come back to life like Lazarus jumping up out of the tomb. Gotta be something electrical, probably a loose or bare wire somewhere. I just have to find the guilty wires and tape them buggers up good and tight."

With a huff, Flo snorted. "The wires in that truck are just fine. A new wiper motor is what is needed. He could save us all a bunch of trouble if he would just drive over to Jake's shop in Eagle Nest and fix it right."

Placing a finger over his lips in a signal for silence, Ernie placed a cupped hand behind one ear before he whispered, "Shhh! I think a crazy person is talking." Ernie slowly looked to the sky and back to the ground as if he were summoning extraterrestrial patience. "If I took this truck into the shop for repairs every time Spud here offers her opinion, there wouldn't be a nickel left in our pockets to raise a cow or run the ranch."

Juanita had told Brad that everyone in the county referred to her aunt simply as Flo, a shortcut for her real name of Florence. Everyone except for Ernie. For as long as anyone could remember, he had called his wife Spud. No one knew the reason or the meaning for the name but that is just what Ernie chose to call his wife.

Stomping her foot and with a head gesture for the rest to follow, Flo grabbed Brad's arm and began marching toward the house. "Come on. I've got iced tea brewed, fresh strawberries right out of my garden and cream in the fridge. What are you all waiting for?" Casting a withering glance to her husband, Flo proclaimed, "If we stand around waiting for my dearest here to fix the wipers on that useless old truck, we might very well still be here when snow flies and folks are singing Christmas carols."

———

Breeze and shade made for a perfect morning on the porch where Ernie, Juanita, and Brad lounged. Returning to her guests after carrying empty dishes into the kitchen, Flo spoke to her husband. "Ernie, have you mentioned what Clifford told you about what happened early this morning?"

"Nope, I'm so damned upset that I hate to ruin this beautiful day by even talking about it." With a shake of his head, Ernie spoke softly. "Sickening. Absolutely sickening."

"Uncle Ernie, what happened?" Juanita looked with concern, first to Flo and then back to Ernie.

"Okay, I'll tell you the whole story. But I'm warning you, what you are about to hear will steam the blood in your veins to a boil." Ernie gathered his thoughts as Flo again seated herself next to her husband and patted his hand.

His voice somber, Ernie began to speak. "Our neighbor up the road, Clifford Taylor, his ranch meets ours and we share a common fence line. He was out this morning, right at sunrise, heading to check on some cattle. He had the road all to himself and was just making his turn onto the cattle guard that leads to his pasture when he darned near got run over by a couple of idiots in a big, red pickup. They were driving like demons from hell and Clifford had to run off into the ditch to keep from getting clobbered. He wanted to go after whoever it was, but by the time he managed to turn around and get back on the road, the pickup was long gone. He knew it was hopeless, so he didn't even try."

Flo spoke up. "Clifford said that if they would have hit him, he would probably be with the saints right now. They were going that fast."

Frustration simmered in Ernie's voice as he continued. "Clifford wasn't sure exactly what was going on but he sure as heck knew something was out of line. He headed on up the road and as he drove, he began to get a feeling of exactly what had happened. He told me that as he drove, he can't say if he felt more angry or more sick."

All eyes focused on Ernie as he paused. "Man-oh-man, does this ever piss me off." Following a sigh of exasperation, Ernie continued. "Clifford headed straight to where a natural spring keeps a small pond filled with fresh water and the land around it remains saturated. Years ago, Clifford planted a few apple trees there just for the beauty and to give a treat to deer and all the animals that roam the ranch."

Brad closed his eyes as he intuitively recognized where this story was going.

"Clifford got out of his truck and walked to the spring. It only took a few seconds for him to spot a blood trail leading away from the pond. Of course, Clifford followed the blood, not really wanting to see where it would lead. He didn't have to go more than a few feet after entering the tree line until he found the freshly decapitated body of a beautiful buck. An arrow wound was obvious in the deer's chest but there was no arrow." Ernie breathed deeply. "Some asshole just left one of God's beautiful creations lying there. Left it to rot."

Ernie became quiet and no one spoke. "That's really it," Ernie continued with a shrug. "Clifford said he immediately drove over to Porter Truman's place. Porter has been the veterinarian around here for years and operates his clinic out of his house. Everybody just calls him Doc Truman. Clifford told Doc Truman about what had happened. The Doc said that there has been a recent rash of poaching all the way from Taos, up through the canyon, and into the Moreno Valley. Elk and deer mostly. But some bear also. Doc Truman figured right away that this was another instance.

"Clifford and Doc Truman drove back to the spring where the deer had been killed. They wanted to take a look around. Sure enough, with just a little bit of poking and looking, they spotted a game camera attached to a tree that gave a perfect view of the spring and pond. Unless someone was really looking, the darned camera would never have been noticed."

"This is horrible." Juanita stood up and walked to her uncle. Bending over, she kissed the top of his head. "I'm so sorry, Uncle Ernie. And I remember meeting Clifford sometime back. He is a prince of a man who loves his ranch and loves this land. What a terrible thing to have happen on his ranch." She paused. "Actually, one could say it happened right in his home."

"Yep. It is very much his home. Every acre of this valley is home to all of us. Fence lines don't mean a thing when it comes to something like this. Having such a slaughter happen so close to any of us stinks to high heaven."

"Did you leave the camera on the tree?" Brad asked.

Ernie shook his head. "No, we carefully removed it. Doc Truman knows the game warden for the area. He's going to hand it over to the Game Department. Hopefully it will help in some way. Who knows, maybe there might be a photo of the asshole who put it on the tree." Ernie shrugged. "Fingerprints maybe. Sim card. I have no idea how long the camera had been out there."

"I don't suppose Clifford saw the license tag on the truck."

"Naw. Everything happened mighty fast. Clifford was trying hard not to get himself killed by the crazy bastards. All he can remember is that it was a big, fancy pickup, bright red. Clifford said it had one of those big-ass cabs that can hold a backseat full of people or a backseat full of crap. Clifford told me he was going to give a statement to the game warden today but there isn't much more to tell them."

"You said bastards, plural. Did Clifford get a look at the driver or anyone else in the truck?" Brad asked the question with hope in his voice.

"Two white guys. The driver had a big ugly beard. Clifford said it looked to him like the guy had just crawled out of hole in the ground. That's all Clifford could tell Doc Truman and that's what he will tell the Game Department when they talk."

No one spoke for a few moments. Sipping tea and thinking, everyone processed Ernie's story in their own way. Brad broke the time of reflection with a solemn voice. "I have no idea how a person could be so depraved. It's hard for me to get my head around something so sick happening here in this beautiful valley."

"I understand your feelings, but don't let the beauty of this area fool you." Ernie grunted. "During the days of the Wild West, this whole area was one rough and tumble place to live. Cimmaron, just over the ridge here," Ernie pointed, "considered it a quiet week if only one or two gun battles or killings took place. And then, just up the road, there is an old ghost town settlement that was known as Elizabeth Town. Back in the day, some guy named Charles Kennedy opened up an inn for travelers." Ernie chuckled. "The old codger turned out to not be very hospitable as he ended up killing somewhere around fourteen of his guests. After murdering the poor souls, he buried their bodies in shallow graves all around the inn. A bunch of vigilantes finally figured out what was going on. They saddled up and took a ride out to Elizabeth Town for a late-night visit to the good Mr. Kennedy. They either strung him up or dragged him to death. The story goes both ways." Ernie paused. Casting a serious look to his audience he spoke with authority. "So, folks, after the events of this morning on Clifford's ranch, I'm thinking we haven't progressed as much as we like to think."

"Oh, I hear you," Brad replied. "But still, every time I hear of something like this, no amount of history or perspective makes it any better. Whoever killed that deer and left it lying like that, they deserve to be strung up or dragged to death just like the innkeeper guy."

A murmur of agreement rippled as Juanita began to gather the tea glasses. "Okay, folks, thank you for your hospitality and strawberries but we must hit the road and leave both of you to important business." Smiling at Ernie, Juanita continued. "That mean brother of yours, I think his name is Foster, demands that I be in the shop this afternoon. He has no idea how to run the business without my supervision. Plus, I happen to know that your preacher is coming for dinner tonight and poor Flo here has a ton of cooking to do."

Ernie stood and kicked at his chair. "Oh, hell yes, the preacher is coming for dinner. What a surprise. He never comes at any time but dinner time. That man is full of shit as a Christmas goose. I can tell you beyond doubt, he don't give a rat's ass about my poor ol' soul. What he does care about is Flo's fried chicken and gravy. You should see how he carries on. And it's all baloney. Here's exactly what's going to happen. We'll sit down at the table this evening with chicken, potatoes, gravy, and all the fixin's steaming hot and smelling like heaven itself. But of course, we have to pray first. He'll commence to talking to God, thanking him for the bounty, asking to nourish our bodies so we can offer glory and adoration. Then it's more hooey about bless our loved ones, forgive our iniquities, count our blessings. Oh my gosh, he goes on and on. My stomach is growling, my ass is itching but that windbag just keeps on a prayin' and a prayin'." Ernie's voice now in a crescendo concluded. "Praise the Lord and pass the ammunition, let's eat for crying out loud!"

Flo, trying not to laugh, spoke calmly. "Careful, Ernie, he's the one who will send you off to glory on the other side when he preaches your funeral. Better stay in his good graces."

Aware that he was entertaining the people gathered on his porch, Ernie's eyes twinkled as he delivered a final proclamation. "Now, you listen to me, Spud. You can tell that holy-roller preacher that I want to be buried upside down. That way when he comes to the cemetery to pray over my dead bones, he can kiss my ass."

Shaking with laughter, Juanita approached her uncle and placed her arms about his shoulders, bringing him into a tight embrace.

"You will live forever, Uncle Ernie. The good Lord certainly won't have you and you would drive that Lucifer guy nuts in less than a day. You just stay right here on this ranch for all eternity so I can always drop by for a visit. Whenever I need strawberries and a hug, I want to come right here to see you and Aunt Flo."

With laughter and hugs, goodbyes were exchanged. Juanita and Brad walked to their vehicle with Flo and Ernie in perfect step. Before driving away, Brad extended his head from behind the wheel of his truck. "Hey, Ernie, I have a favor to ask. Please let me know of anything you hear about the killing of that deer. I really want to know if the investigation makes any progress."

With a thumbs up and a farewell wave, Ernie acknowledged Brad's request. "You got it."

———

Comfortable silence took the place of music for several minutes as Juanita and Brad retraced their route along the Enchanted Circle. Finally, Juanita spoke what was on both their minds. "So much for wondering about your feelings this morning. I have no explanation but neither do I have any doubt; somehow, someway, the horrible slaughter of that deer is exactly what delivered your premonition of something being terribly wrong." Brad gave a slight nod of agreement but did not speak.

Staring through the windshield, Juanita's mind was far outside the truck's cab as she continued. "I believe every word you say when you tell me how you are certain that you first met me in some sort of dream in which I was living in another time. And I know just as certainly that, when I first laid eyes on you, every fiber of my soul shouted that I knew everything about you, and that we were intended to be together." Juanita reached for Brad's hand. "I don't know, Brad. What happened? How were we so mysteriously brought together?" Juanita pressed harder into Brad's hand. "Should we just feel wonderfully blessed or should we both be a bit frightened?"

Lost in his own memories of the past, Brad did not speak but returned the pressure of Juanita's grip. His mind had drifted into a world of wonderment that he visited more frequently than he cared to admit. After he had taken early retirement from the FBI to be with his dying wife, circumstances had repeatedly thrust him into webs of evil and mystery. One such instance, involving white supremacists set on a mission of revenge, led to a brutal assault that almost took his life. While recovering from the attack, he had experienced dreams, or visions, of being cared for by a woman in a different time and different place. Brad had no idea how to explain what he knew within his mind and heart, but he was certain that the woman who cared for him in the dream was Juanita. The morphing of dream into the reality of his current life created an ocean of mystery. His passion for the woman now seated next to him was forever embedded within the fog of that mystery.

Keeping her gaze outside the cab of the truck, Juanita continued speaking. Her words were spoken as much to herself as to Brad. "When Uncle Ernie told us about the senseless killing of that deer, it was déjà vu. The mystery of how we came together hit me again. How did we meet in another world? How did you feel this morning's evil after an owl awakened you? How did you sense something that happened miles away?"

Brad offered no reply as he drove. Eyes straight ahead, his silence stoic.

"I'm convinced that it's all the same forces in play here. Because of unexplained intuition on your part, you uncovered a plot of revenge on the part of some really bad people. Those bad people tried to kill you. Because someone tried to take your life, you and I found each other." Juanita's voice softened as she turned to look at Brad. "Is it happening again? Your feelings from this morning are what led us to Uncle Ernie's story. Something inside me is saying loud and clear that things aren't going to end with that deer." Uneasy quiet filled the truck's cab. "Something is going on here, Brad. How or why do these things keep happening to us? Who is talking to us?"

The hum of tires on pavement was the only response to Juanita's wonderings. They both knew there were no answers. However, within the murky waters of so much that was beyond explanation, something new now swirled. The morning's premonitions of evil were crystalized. The image of the carcass of a beautiful deer, head severed, and lifeless body left as a feast to flies and scavengers now rode as a passenger in the truck.

———

After stopping for fuel, Brad parked his truck in front of the gift shop. With a peck on Juanita's cheek, he spoke. "Enjoy the afternoon working with your uncle. I'm going to shoot over to Taos for an early dinner with Hank." With a grin of mischief on his face, Brad continued. "That goofy guy is the only fishing guide I know who manages to fall into the river just about every time he goes near a stream. If falling into a river should ever become an official Olympic event, Hank will be on the podium, scratching and grinning, accepting a gold medal. I have no idea how he makes a living as a guide other than the fact that he is hilarious entertainment."

"Hush your nonsense. I could never, ever forget Hank. He is far more handsome than you and he has better table manners. Tell him that I still have a crush on him and look forward to our next secret rendezvous."

"You are a total snit, my dear. Go rendezvous with your Uncle Foster. Unless I get a better offer, you can expect me back a little after dark."

"Okay, you are on your own. Behave and enjoy an enchilada for me." Juanita swung her body out of the truck. Placing fingertips to lips, she tossed a kiss as she walked to the gift shop.

Once again, Brad drove the Enchanted Circle. Only this time, he traveled in the opposite direction from the morning's trip with Juanita. His route would take him west, through the village of Questa, before a southward plunge into Taos. He looked forward to that portion of the drive as it paralleled the mountain range that is home to the Taos Indian Pueblo and Reservation. Towering above the vastness of New Mexico, ever-changing light and sky conditions made the mountains seem alive. Brad felt as though they exhaled cool breath over land lying seven thousand feet above the oceans. On most evenings, sunset brought the glow of a ripe orange. Brad loved this portion of New Mexico. In his mind, it absolutely was the Land of Enchantment.

Glad to be alone for a while, Brad used the time to think things over. The day's events had rekindled memories of past experiences that had taken him into some dark places. Each of those experiences had involved the same sense of ominousness that he had felt with this early morning's visit from an owl outside his window. Brad gazed at the mountains drifting past the window of his truck. He inhaled the air. This was the Land of Enchantment. But thoughts of the morning's carnage and the pointless death of a beautiful animal would not leave his mind. His whisper remained within the truck: "I'm sure as heck not feeling very enchanted today."

———

The image of a mustachioed skeletal figure, adorned in a sombrero and serape, welcomed Brad to what he considered the best Mexican food in Taos. Umbrellas brightened the café's patio in festive splashes of color. Laughter and the buzz of happy chatter brought a smile to his face. Lifting mugs of Santa Fe Pale Ale, Hank and Brad toasted before savoring a long draw. A satisfied sigh followed as both men sat back in relaxation. "If the Good Lord made anything better than this place, he kept it for himself." Brad took another draw, pleased with his pronouncement.

Nodding in agreement and with another satisfied sigh, Hank responded. "If it weren't for having to make a living, I would just let this patio be my home. Right here under this very umbrella could be my permanent address. With a beer in my hand, of course." Hank grinned and again sipped the amber drink. Hank exhibited the physical appearance of one who lived an outdoor life to its fullest. Graying hair, just touching his ears, was tucked beneath a sweat-stained baseball cap emblazoned with an image of a rainbow trout. A suntanned face and piercing eyes now bore the burden of needing reading glasses. But Hank carried his cross with dignity. When he peered over his cheater glasses, perpetually rosy cheeks and a twisted smile glowed. People in Hank's presence were left uncertain if he remained on the verge of laughing with them or laughing at them.

The men made small talk, catching up on life, as they consumed blue corn enchiladas, pinto beans, posole, and chile rellenos. Hank and Brad had initially met while fishing on a small trout stream on the New Mexico-Colorado border. Their personalities had synchronized, and friendship solidified through passing years. Working as a fishing guide, Hank was intimately familiar with the rivers, streams and mountains from Santa Fe to the Colorado border.

Afternoon light faded as they dined. Savoring the ambiance and peacefulness that follows a meal of quality shared with valued friends, Hank and Brad held on to the moment. Evening's cool drifted down from the Sangre de Cristo Mountains as they lingered over coffee, faintly tinged with the flavor of piñon. The appreciation both men felt for the serenity of the moment did not need to be mentioned.

"I need to run something by you." Brad spoke with a hint of somberness in his voice. "Juanita and I heard a story this morning and it's really bothering me. I just can't shake it." Brad did not mention the other unsettling feelings that also weighed on his and Juanita's minds.

"Fire away." Hank coddled his coffee mug in both hands and was quiet.

"Juanita has an aunt and uncle who own a ranch just a few miles from Eagle Nest. We paid them a visit this morning and her uncle told us about something that had just happened on a bordering ranch." Brad related the story of the near collision on a country road and a poached and decapitated deer left to rot. "I understand that these things happen with more frequency than we care to think about, but this despicable act, right here under my nose, is tough for me to stomach."

Hank placed his coffee on the table. "Of course, it's tough to stomach. Any sane person who has even minimal respect for nature, or for life itself, finds people who do that stuff repugnant." Hank shook his head. "But there are plenty of assholes out there who sure as heck aren't sane."

Hank leaned forward over the table. "I'm glad you told me about this. I stay in touch with fishing guides and outfitters all over this area. We talk on a regular basis and share information about water conditions, fire dangers, and that sort of stuff. I also have friends who are game wardens or work with the Department of Fish and Wildlife in various capacities. They tell me that there has recently been an unusually high amount of poaching going on throughout northern New Mexico and into Colorado. They are asking for help from fishing guides to be alert for this. They suspect the poachers set up what appears to be a legitimate fishing camp for cover, but the real reason is to scout the area for poaching opportunities. They use sophisticated camera gear to monitor wildlife trails and areas of frequent use. Then, they bait areas with grain or easy food for a quick and easy kill. Sometimes, to attract bears, the bastards put out piles of old pastries or slabs of bacon. Then they lie in wait for their opportunity. They are lawless and ruthless. Not to mention cruel as hell. They bait, trap, poison, and maim without conscience."

A shake of the head was Brad's response before muttering, "Really tough, brave guys."

"Yeah, exactly the kind of scumbags you want to have over for supper. But don't kid yourself. Those shitbirds make a lot of money. Rich folks will pay big bucks for so-called guided hunts to bag a guaranteed trophy. Sometimes, the hunt is not even necessary. Lots of fat-ass, outdoor-wannabe types will fork over big bucks for a head or rack of a game animal. It must improve their testosterone level to hang a purchased trophy in their fancy-ass library or office. The travesty of how all this comes together is of no concern to those bastards."

"Manly men!"

"No shit." Hank made a circling motion with his arms as he continued. "We're talking a vast area here and much of it really rugged territory. You've got federal government land and state-owned land mixed in with private property. A very small number of enforcement folks is all that exists to police gazillions of square miles. They have an impossible job." Hank peered over the top of his glasses as he sipped from his coffee mug. "And believe me, a poor ranger who ends up face to face with those shitbirds is in a dangerous position. Every year rangers and wardens are assaulted and sometimes murdered by those testosterone-fueled shitheads."

"I understand what they are up against." Brad was thoughtful as he leaned back. "I'm not sure what good it will do but this morning's sighting of a big, red pickup truck might prove to be significant. My guess is that whoever was driving that vehicle is smart enough to realize they were spotted and won't be cruising around the area in plain sight. If they have a camp somewhere, they will probably park the truck and use other vehicles for a while."

"Yeah, I suspect you are correct. The best thing I know to do is to put the word out to the network of guides to be alert for a fishing camp that has a red truck sitting around. It's a long shot, but who knows. During this time of year, guides are stomping around all over God's green earth with clients, so maybe somebody will see something." Hank gave a shrug. "Worth a try."

"Sounds good to me." Brad cast a smug grin as he continued. "If you can keep your wrinkled ass from falling into the river long enough to look around a bit, maybe you can spot the truck and finally make yourself useful."

Hank rose from his chair. "I have no interest in your abuse. I'm outta here 'cause I'm driving back to Santa Fe and it's going to be dark soon." Extending his hand, he spoke again. "Give Juanita my best." Shaking his head in wonderment, Hank concluded as he prepared to walk away. "And tell that beautiful woman I will never, ever understand what she sees in you."

———

The sun was below the horizon by the time Brad passed through Questa on his return trip. As events of the day passed through his mind as he drove, he considered how his time with Hank had delivered a sense of tranquility. Knowing that Juanita waited for him in their room above Foster's shop, Brad whispered a prayer of gratitude. He thanked the heavens for friendship. He thanked the heavens for the unexplained mystery of whatever had happened to bring Juanita and him together.

Stars sprinkled the sky as Brad pulled his truck to the parking area behind the gift shop. He quietly ascended the steps leading to the private living quarters, inserted his key, and spoke softly as he entered. "Hey, princess, I'm back. No point in resisting. I'm going to take you away. You shall be mine forever and forever."

Holding a book in her hands, Juanita was sitting upright in bed. Freshly showered, her hair fell about her shoulders as shadows. Copper-colored skin and dark eyes glowed in the dim light of her reading lamp. Just as had happened a million times before, Brad felt his heart skip. He sucked a quick breath. Transfixed in the doorway, eyes locked on Juanita, Brad spoke in a whisper. "Oh, my God! You are so beautiful."

"And you are so easy." Juanita's soft laugh as she spoke cast a hint of enticement into her words. Placing the book on the pillow beside her, she seductively crooked her index finger. "Come over here, handsome stranger, I need you to be much closer."

Aware that he carried a foolish grin, Brad moved to Juanita, sat on the edge of her bed, and kissed her softly.

A smile gleamed within Juanita's eyes. "You don't have to tell me a thing. Your kiss betrays all, my love. You had blue corn enchiladas, posole, and Santa Fe Pale Ale."

"Guilty as charged, counselor. I confess, plead guilty, and beg for mercy." They both laughed before Brad took her hand to hold as he asked about her afternoon in the shop with her Uncle Foster.

"A piece of cake and absolutely fun. Business was steady and I always learn things just by listening to Uncle Foster as he talks with people about Native American pottery and jewelry. That man is a walking encyclopedia."

Shaking his head in agreement, Brad spoke. "Yep, that he is. It makes me happy that you have enjoyed your time here. However, young lady, what in the world are you going to do when this little vacation is over, and you find yourself back in the courtroom?"

"Don't be so certain I'm going back, Mr. Know-It-All. I told you this morning that I'm liking this life. You just may have to find yourself a new bread winner." Lifting her eyebrows in an inquisitive gesture, Juanita concluded, "Now, exactly what are your plans if I declare myself a liberated woman?"

Rising from the bed, Brad gave a dismissive wave. "I'll think it over in the shower, figure things out, and give you my plan."

After showering, Brad turned out the lights and slipped into bed beside Juanita. They lay beside each other, holding hands in silence. Rolling to place her head on Brad's shoulder, Juanita spoke. "Hey, I forgot to mention something. This afternoon while I was busy with a customer, a man came in to see Uncle Foster. He brought a piece of pottery that he wants authenticated and evaluated. Uncle Foster told the guy he didn't really do that type of thing, but the man was quite insistent. They went back and forth for a few minutes and finally Uncle Foster gave in. After taking a photograph of the pottery, Uncle Foster printed off a detailed receipt that he gave to the guy. The man will stay in touch for Uncle Foster's opinion."

"Sounds a little strange," Brad grunted.

"Uncle Foster was definitely agitated by the time the man left. He said he had a really bad feeling about the whole thing. The pottery is obviously genuine and very valuable. Uncle Foster was convinced that the man knows nothing about the history or the value of what he has. Plus, the guy was very vague about how it had come into his possession." Juanita gave a lighthearted laugh. "A smelly-ass rat is how Uncle Foster described the whole thing."

"The perils of having knowledge, I suppose. What's your uncle going to do?"

"I don't know. He said he wants to think it over but it's bothering him, I can tell. Uncle Foster wants to talk things over with both of us tomorrow."

"He can talk forever but I don't know Native American pottery from Chinese fruit cake."

Extending her fingers, Juanita gave a pinch to Brad's arm. "Chinese fruit cake may be every bit as good as enchiladas for all you know. Now, before you fall asleep, do me a favor. It's too warm in here. How about opening the window for us?"

"Yes, your highness. Anything to make life more comfortable for you." An arc of moon cast just enough light for Brad to find the handle and crank open the window. As the window opened, Brad sucked a deep breath. Only feet away, on the branch of a ponderosa pine tree, an owl was perched. Unperturbed by the opening of the window, oval eyes peered into Brad's face in an unwavering, silent stare.

# FOUR

The small kitchen area that served the upstairs bedroom and living area above the gift shop provided a cozy fit for Foster, Juanita, and Brad. Foster had called earlier explaining that he would appreciate some time to talk before opening for business. He had arrived, cheerfully announcing that the bag he carried was filled with freshly made donuts from a nearby bakery. Juanita enjoyed small bites with a fork while Foster and Brad, using their fingers as shovels, shamelessly stuffed their mouths.

Looking in amazement at her uncle before shifting her gaze to Brad, Juanita spoke with feigned aggravation. "Excuse me! I hate to interrupt this gluttonous frenzy, but I do think my uncle has something to talk about beyond donuts. Can you both lick your fingers, wipe your faces, sip some coffee, and then maybe, just maybe, settle down for a bit of civilized conversation before the clock strikes nine? Uncle Foster and I must go downstairs to the shop and actually conduct business with the public. It would be nice if this could happen without donut glaze smeared over my uncle's face and hands." Following a scathing glance, and with a roll of her eyes, Juanita continued. "Not to mention, what's already splotched all over both of your shirts."

Tossing a guilty-as-charged glance across the table to Brad, Foster shrugged his shoulders. "Well, hell, I guess I did have a reason for coming over here bright and early, but these donuts made me lose my senses. Whatever was on my mind, I have completely forgotten and don't even care if I remember."

With a humph of disgust, but her eyes smiling, Juanita stepped to the coffeemaker and returned to fill emptied mugs. Taking her seat, she simply looked at each man, expectancy on her face.

"Okay, my little niece, you sure know how to ruin a party. But I suppose you are right. I need to talk with you both about what happened yesterday."

Leaning back into his chair, Brad spoke. "Juanita told me just a little about some strange character coming into the shop. But I don't have a good picture. How about you just tell the whole story."

"Fair enough." Foster sipped coffee as he gathered his thoughts. "It was well into the afternoon when this really big guy comes walking into the shop. With just a glance, I knew for sure he wasn't a regular tourist." Foster shrugged. "I don't know how to explain it because we get all types in the shop. But this guy just didn't fit. He was shaggy looking, both in clothing and general appearance. Know what I mean? It was pretty warm out yesterday, but this guy was wearing jeans that had to be hot as the dickens. The jeans were dirty, all faded out and ragged. But they were ragged from wear, not the Gucci kind that idiots pay a fortune for these days. You know, because they want them to look worn out."

Juanita and Brad both smiled in understanding.

"His shirt was long-sleeved and a heavy-duty material. It was more like what a construction person would wear, but sure as heck not someone looking to browse a gift shop. His boots and everything about him looked like a man who spent time outdoors. He hadn't shaved in days and the hair sticking out from under his cap looked ratty as the dickens. But I'm no fool and I learned long ago not to judge a book by its cover. In the gift business, looks can quite often be deceiving."

Once again, Juanita and Brad smiled.

"So, Juanita was busy helping a customer and I was behind the counter. The guy just stands and looks around for a few seconds, like he was figuring out what to do next. He took a pretty long look at Juanita before he walked across the store to me. So, I've already figured out that I don't like this guy. He seemed uncomfortable in his facial expression and body language, like he didn't know what to do or what to say. I turned on my phony charm and asked if I could help him with anything in particular. The guy kinda hesitated and didn't say anything. Then I realized he was holding something in his hands, something wrapped up in an old towel. Without saying a word, he unwraps the towel and shows me a piece of pottery. He just held it for a bit before finally opening his mouth to tell me he wants my opinion of what it was worth. He then proceeds to put the pottery on the counter and simply stare at me with a really intense look."

Foster looked to Juanita and Brad with a questioning expression. "Now, I am wondering if the guy is about to whack me over the head and rob me of everything I have or is he serious about wanting my thoughts on the pottery. I did my best to stay calm and friendly and explained to the guy that I have some knowledge of pottery but I sure as heck don't claim to be an expert. He just shook his head without saying a word and kept on staring at me. Good Lord, he was creepy. I went on to explain that I have developed a relationship with a few potters here in northern New Mexico and I can converse intelligently about the basic aspects of their works. But that's it. I don't know the really old stuff and my eye is not trained to spot a sophisticated fraud. I told him that I deal in legitimate pieces crafted by current local artists who I personally know. That's the way I do business and that's it."

Foster took a break from his story for a sip of coffee and Juanita took the opportunity to speak. "What do you think he was showing you, Uncle Foster? Was it really something valuable?"

"Well, I'm not absolutely positive. But my instinct and limited knowledge tell me that it's probably valuable. In fact, I suspect it is very valuable. In the thousands maybe. I'm not comfortable in putting a figure on it and that is exactly what I told the guy. I was totally honest with him about my level of expertise. There were faded markings on the bottom of the piece. Maybe a signature of some sort that would probably mean something to a genuine expert. I told the guy I was not qualified to verify the legitimacy of the markings or anything else about what he had."

"What did he say to you?" Brad asked.

"The guy said he wanted me to go to the experts or visit big galleries on his behalf and determine the value of what he has. He said he would pay me for my time."

"This sounds goofy," Juanita said. She crossed her legs and scowled.

"I asked how he had come into possession of the pottery, and he gave me a baloney line about how it was payment for work he had done for someone. It was a BS answer, I'm certain."

"Juanita told me last night that you ended up keeping the pottery and telling the guy you would try to help him."

"Yeah. I guess curiosity killed the cat," Foster replied. "If it's genuine, he was showing me an interesting piece of pottery. If it's a fraud, it's still interesting. I'm willing to explore a bit to see what I can learn. I took photographs, wrote out a description, and put it all into a receipt for the guy. He said he will check back in a couple of weeks to see what I've learned."

"Are you telling me that he just left the pottery with you? Did he give you instructions or a way to contact him?"

"You've got it," Foster replied. "It was obvious that he did not want to divulge any personal information to me. I told him that I would not consider doing this without some idea of who I was dealing with. The guy was squirming like a hooker in church, but he finally agreed to show me a Utah driver's license. His name is Luther Birdwell. I have a photograph of the license."

Leaning over the table, Foster rubbed his brow in thought. "I'm second guessing myself for getting involved with this. The two of you have a bunch of experience with shady characters so I value your opinions. Juanita, you prosecute cases involving all kinds of scoundrels." Looking at Brad, Foster grinned. "And as for you, Mr. Walker, if I'm to believe half of what my niece tells me, years in the FBI gave you quite an education in horse thieves and outlaws. If either of you have insight, I'm all ears." Foster lifted his arms in a gesture of frustration. "After the guy left, I put the pottery in my safe. Maybe I should just leave it there until he returns. I'm happy to say that I can't help him and give the darned thing back."

Exchanging looks, Juanita and Brad simultaneously shrugged. Brad spoke. "Look, Foster, this is way out of my league and anything I say is simply shooting from the hip. But I can tell you that the whole thing sounds bizarre. I think you are absolutely right to be suspicious. I don't know anything at all about how to authenticate pottery but I'm happy to call an old police officer friend. It's worth a shot to see if anything can be learned from the Utah license the guy gave you."

Juanita followed Brad's comment. "I'm with Brad. This is not my area of expertise. However, I know that our Albuquerque office from time to time prosecutes cases involving various forms of illegal activity involving exploitation of Native American artifacts. Thefts that include valuable works of art or artifacts happen from time to time. I am friends with the prosecutor who has some experience in these cases. I'm happy to give her a call and see what she has to say."

Brad spoke next. "I have to ask this, even though I doubt you can answer. Did you by any chance get a look at what the guy was driving?"

"Don't be so skeptical." Foster smiled as he replied. "I didn't just fall off the turnip truck last night. I walked over to the window after he left, hoping to see what he was driving. I watched him walk about a block up the street. He got into a black pickup truck with a camper shell. That's all I can tell you though. I wasn't able to catch a look at the license plate."

"Better than nothing," Brad replied.

"I would appreciate your help with anything the two of you can do." Foster stood. "Well, I suppose I should go get the shop ready for opening." He glanced at the bag still containing an uneaten donut. "It's a sin to leave a fresh donut on the table but I'm walking away." He smiled a mischievous smile. "Also, if you want to know the truth, I really have very few ideas about how to verify the authenticity or value of the pot. I kinda gave the guy some hooey 'cause I'm just curious." Foster chuckled as he left the room. "But that will remain our little secret."

————

Ignoring Juanita and the barrage of insults she hurled concerning his donut breakfast of champions, Brad settled into the quiet of their living space. Before placing a call to his friend Sam Trathen, he enjoyed a few moments of reflection. Sam was both a police officer and a treasured friend. Not only had he and Sam worked cases together for years, but Sam had also been a rock of support when premature death had taken Brad's wife, Elizabeth. Closing his eyes, Brad remembered those dark days. Sam had been there through it all. He had hugged Brad, counseled his three children, and held them all together when despair ravaged their lives.

Casting his eyes to the ceiling, Brad also recalled how it had been Sam who had been first to recognize Juanita's entrance into Brad's life. It had been Sam who offered encouragement for him to allow love back into his world. It was Sam who assured him that Elizabeth smiled from heaven when thoughts and images of Juanita had begun to stir within Brad's heart and mind. Unconsciously moving his head, Brad offered a silent prayer of gratitude that he had been blessed with a friend of such character and substance.

Sam answered on the third ring. "What the heck you calling about this time? You chasing child traffickers or rolling around in the mud with a naked goofball in the middle of a rainstorm?"

Unable to come up with a rapid or clever response, Brad could only laugh. Memories of the events that Sam referred to would last a lifetime. They had been terrifying at the time but now provided fodder for friendly ridicule and tons of laughter. "Whatever you do, don't say hello or ask how I'm doing, you old coot. Just start off with your usual insults."

Following moments of banter and reminiscing about a recent fly-fishing trip in Canada that they had shared, Brad related to Sam the story of the slaughtered and decapitated deer.

"There just ain't no end to the assholes, Brad. Not enough police or jail cells to keep the bastards in check. They propagate like rabbits." Sam hesitated. "Or like roaches is a better way to put it."

After agreeing with Sam's evaluation, Brad got down to business. The description of yesterday's visitor to the gift shop and his request produced a chuckle from Sam. "You know something, Brad? I think that metal plate that serves as your skull must be a magnet that attracts whackos. There is simply no other explanation for how so many crazy people find you." Sam laughed again. "Okay, let me guess. You need me to do a little research on this guy based on his Utah driver's license."

"You catch on fast. Anything you can find will be appreciated and remembered with an expensive gift on your next birthday."

"Yeah, right. I'm stepping into an interview that's going to last a while. Once I'm clear of that, I'll hop right on this and give you a ring as soon as I can."

After exchanging final barbs, Brad disconnected from his friend and sat in silence. Where had the years gone? What was coming next? Juanita was struggling with exhaustion from the pressure of endless trials. What was really bothering her was the endless caravan of victims. The tragedy of victims was huge a part of her life. Juanita's heart and mind was not wired to allow separation from the horror of lives devastated by rape, murder, or the myriad of exploitations that were as common for her as morning coffee is for most people.

Brad thought again of Sam. What sort of interview was he conducting? Whatever he was dealing with, it was a sure bet that at the end of the story lay the damaged or destroyed life of a victim.

Behind Brad's closed eyes, a portrait took shape. A smeared canvas, streaks of grotesque. A decapitated deer. Flies. Rot. An innocent creature simply seeking a drink of water. Not all victims were human.

———

Afternoon clouds thickened. Thunder rolled across the sky, sweeping over the highest peaks of the mountains before tumbling into the village of Red River. Streets that had been bustling with tourists and shoppers were quickly becoming deserted. Sporadic rain drops splattered as gusting winds gathered strength. Dust and bits of trash swirled through the air like confetti as straggling shoppers made frantic dashes for cover. The warning was clear, especially to people familiar with life in the mountains. The brewing storm would probably be short, but it meant business.

Foster had left the shop early, leaving Juanita alone to handle business. Seated in a rocker on the gift shop's covered porch, protected and dry, Brad enjoyed one of his favorite pleasures. Mother Nature displaying her power and beauty was an experience that both fascinated and humbled. Gently rocking, he settled in for the afternoon's performance.

Vibration of his cell phone interrupted the moment. The low growl of Sam Trathen's voice reminded Brad of the thunder that rumbled through the sky. "Okay, sunshine, modern technology is a mystery, but by golly, it sometimes serves us well. Thanks to the magic of computers, I found some interesting stuff on your Utah boy, Luther Birdwell. You ready?"

From his shirt pocket, Brad retrieved a pen, along with a glaze-covered napkin that had held the morning's last donut. "Fire away." Using the arm of his wooden rocker as a pad, Brad prepared to take notes.

"Luther is a stellar citizen. The kind of guy you would love to see your daughter bring home. His cover story is that he markets himself as guide for big game hunts. But peel the onion back a bit, and the truth is not a pretty picture. About five years ago, Luther was the focus of a multi-state investigation involving poaching and all kinds of wildlife and game violations. He conducted so-called hunts that were rigged, or he illegally killed big game animals himself. After his taxidermist did the devil's work, Birdwell got big money for the head that he sold to clients."

"Holy shit." Brad's mind recalled Ernie's story of the poached deer. Yesterday's conversation with Hank sounded again.

"Yep, I think your holy shit reaction is spot on. Birdwell was arrested and convicted on several counts of illegally baiting, trapping, and poaching animals near Park City, Utah. The investigators were certain that he was guilty of similar crimes in other states, but Utah had the best case, so they ran with it."

"Gotta take it where you can get it."

"He got his ass nailed with a $25,000 fine and two years in the slammer. The report that I have in front of me doesn't say how much time he actually did. There is a darn good chance he was out in less time than the full sentence. Utah suspended all hunting and fishing privileges for a period of ten years." Sam snarled. "Like that kind of shitbird gives a damn about a hunting license."

"This puts a whole different light on his coming into the gift shop. That bastard probably picked up the pottery as payment for a poaching job of some sort and now he isn't sure about what he has."

"That's my guess also. The best way to get the full story on your boy Birdwell is to contact the investigator with Utah Division of Wildlife Service. I can give you his name and contact information."

"Wow! This is great info, Sam. What about address or vehicles?"

"Listen, Brad, I have to run. I have a great lead on a guy I've been looking for. A few weeks ago, the guy robbed a convenience store. Then, just for funsies, he forced the clerk, a young girl, into his car, drove her into a remote area, and raped her. I've got him located in a condo complex. We are off to hook him up and I need to hustle. I'll text you later with all I have about vehicles and addresses but it's all old stuff. Totally obsolete. The important info will be what you can get from the investigator in Utah."

"Of course. Go get the SOB. I'll call Utah right away. Keep your head down, my friend."

Brad folded the napkin and gently rocked, his mind in another world. He seldom spoke about it to others, but his heart ached to be with Sam right now. Nobody but God in heaven knew how much he missed that part of his old life. He inhaled deeply. Closed his eyes. A girl working in a convenience store. Trying to make a living. Robbed. Raped. Another victim.

Absent-mindedly tapping his cell phone on his leg, Brad brought himself back into the present. While talking with Sam, the weather had worsened. Wind gusts were now menacing. rain blew onto the porch carrying the smell of a storm. Thinking of Sam, what he had learned, and dealing with suppressed emotions, Brad did not hear Juanita step from the shop's front door. He was startled when she appeared beside him, touched his shoulder, and whispered his name. "Brad."

Juanita said nothing more but simply stared toward the street with a strange expression on her face. Lightning flashed and thunder rolled. Wind swept under the covered porch. Rain pelted and the shop's windchimes careened. A cacophony of frenzied notes pealed in discord.

"Juanita, what's wrong? Are you okay?" Brad stood, placing his hands on Juanita's shoulders, gazing into her face with concern. "You look awful. Are you ill?"

"What happened to the lady that just left the shop? Where did she go?" A tremor lurked in Juanita's hoarse voice.

"Juanita, I've been sitting right here for a long time. Not a soul has been in or out." He looked to the empty street, gazing up and down in both directions. "I don't think anybody is going to be out in this weather. What are you talking about?"

Simply looking up into Brad's face, Juanita remained silent. Tears began to seep from her eyes, etching a trickle down her cheeks.

"Sweetheart, what in the world is wrong? You are frightening me. Tell me what's happening."

Rain blew harder. The windchimes banged a medley of chaos.

A quiver was now definitely in Juanita's voice. "Brad, please. Are you telling me that you didn't see that lady? She walked right past you when she came into the shop. She talked about you being out here and would have been within inches of you as she entered. And again, when she left, she would have practically touched you." Juanita's tears no longer trickled but flowed. Her body shivered as she collapsed into Brad's embrace.

Mountain peak to valley floor, thunder crashed.

Having no idea what was triggering Juanita's behavior, Brad drew her close, holding tightly as possible. "Come on, sweetheart. We have to go inside. This weather is getting vicious."

Giving a nod, Juanita pulled away from Brad's embrace and

stepped to the doorway. But before entering, she turned, her eyes once more searching the street. Desperate to see through the storm, Juanita stared for several seconds. "She was just here, Brad. She just left. I saw her. I talked with her. She walked right out of this door and into the storm. Oh, my God, Brad. What is happening?" Moving as if she were in a trance, Juanita turned to enter the shop. Collapsing onto the couch that sat beneath the shop's front window, she held her eyes straight ahead. Seconds passed as she sat in silence. Her breathing labored, Juanita was seemingly not even aware of Brad's presence.

"Talk to me, Juanita." Brad sat down, taking one of her hands within his. "Talk to me. What in the world is wrong?"

Juanita's breath eased and her gaze gradually focused on Brad. Brad observed quietly, watching her shoulders relax and a degree of composure return.

Holding her hand, Brad waited, uncertain if he should remain quiet or speak.

Swiping the back of her hand over a tear-steaked face, Juanita finally began to speak, her tone slow and deliberate. "I have never forgotten how you described to me your experience after being attack by the man who took a pipe to your head. In a dream or a vision, whatever it was, you were in a tiny cabin that seemed to be a throwback to frontier days."

"That's right." Brad nodded his head.

"And you told me how a woman took care of you and gave you some sort of healing broth."

Another nod from Brad.

"And you swear that the woman who cared for you was actually me."

"That's right. It sounds impossible. But I know my experience was real. I know in my heart that the woman was you." Brad's shoulders moved and his eyes narrowed. "Every word of that story is true."

"Oh, my God, Brad, it was her. The woman who entered the shop, she looked directly into my eyes and gave me the strangest smile. I almost fainted. I was looking at myself! The mirror image of me stood close enough to touch! She was dressed exactly as you described the woman who cared for you in your vision or dream. After a few seconds, with me just staring speechless, the woman laughed and asked why I was so surprised to see her. I couldn't speak. I think I might have moved my head or shrugged but I honestly can't remember. I think I was in shock."

"Jesus, sweetheart."

Removing her hand from Brad's grip, Juanita leaned forward and placed both hands over her eyes. "I'm trying to remember, Brad, I'm trying. As this was happening, I was desperate to understand what was taking place." Juanita's body shivered. "And now, I still have no idea what in the world happened."

"It's okay. Take your time."

Straightening her body and reaching to again hold Brad's hands, Juanita spoke. "The woman pointed to the clock. The one hanging on the wall behind the counter." Juanita's eyes briefly looked to the clock as if she needed to reassure herself that a clock was actually there. "I can't recall her exact words, but she began talking about how strange it is that people only measure time by the hands of a clock. I remember her saying something about if an hourglass ran empty but if no one was around to turn the glass over, what happened to the time in between. She kept looking at the clock and talking about time. She said something about how wrong it is that people think time only moves in one direction. She wondered why they can't realize that time is nothing more than how a person chooses to see. And then, Brad, she looked straight into my eyes and called me by name. She actually called me Juanita! And what she said, I recall exactly. She pointed a finger at me and said, 'Juanita, of all people, you must learn. It is important for you to understand this.'"

"Silence hung as Juanita paused. Brad sat, stunned.

"I'm probably going to forget something or say her words out of order but here is what I recall. She knew your name also. She said to remind Brad that he was told by the man with a big mustache that it would be Manuel's sister who cared for him. Then she sort of smiled and said 'Why do people see no life in people just because they have left this world? With so many souls out there, don't you think their lives must continue to echo in some manner?' Then she pointed at me again and gave me a stern look before continuing. 'If one pays attention, secrets of life can be found among those things that are thought to be dead. Pay attention, Juanita. Life is everywhere. Do not assume things are dead.'"

"She actually used my name when she talked about a man with a mustache and a man named Manuel?" Brad spoke with disbelief.

"Oh, yes, she absolutely did. In fact, as she spoke your name, she pointed over her shoulder to where you were sitting. She gave me the strangest smile and said something about how the man with the mustache, Manuel, and the famous scout were great friends. She said they speak with each other often."

Brad swallowed hard.

"Then, Brad, the woman's voice changed. She sounded firm, almost harsh. Her face and voice seemed like she was giving me a warning about something. She said to pay attention and be careful because evil was nearby. After saying that, or something close to that, she just turned and walked toward the door. But before leaving she turned and looked right at me. She pointed to me and then pointed to herself. And, this is a quote, Brad, exactly what she said. Her words were, 'You and I are very lucky to be given these chances. Be thankful that you are able to finish the life that was taken from you. Make each day count. Pay attention and make wise decisions. People think that death comes in a moment. They forget that life happens in moments. Pay attention, Juanita. Do not miss your moments.'"

Shrugging her shoulders and lifting her eyes to stare into the ceiling, Juanita became quiet. "That's what she said to me. She told me to not miss my moments."

Color drained from Brad's face, but his eyes never wavered from Juanita. He scarcely breathed. The only sound in the shop came from the ticking clock. Finally, Brad managed to speak, his voice somber. "I've been suspecting that something like this would one day happen. After being assaulted, the experiences I had in the other world were too real. They were not a dream or a vision. They actually happened. A man with a huge mustache put me on a horse and said Manuel's sister would care for me. I was in a primitive cabin. A woman cared for me. And the woman was you, Juanita. She was you."

It was Brad's turn to place both hands over his face as his body rocked. Juanita now waited, giving Brad time. With a deep breath, Brad sat straight and spoke softly. "I'm totally mystified, and I suppose a little bit terrified also. But I'm not surprised. It had to happen, Juanita. It just had to happen."

Juanita nodded her head. "I think I understand, and I feel the same. From the first time I laid eyes on you, every fiber of my being told me I had known you somewhere before. It was more than just a silly feeling to me, but I felt silly talking about it." Juanita moved her head from side to side. "But after what has just happened, it no longer seems silly."

With a sigh, Brad sank back into the couch. "My entire body feels weak. I have no idea what this means or what to do." Seconds of silence passed, both lost in their own thoughts. "Was that it, anything more? What happened after that statement about finishing a life that was taken from you?"

"The woman opened the door and started to leave. She was only inches from where you were sitting. But before she stepped out, she turned again. She seemed to be thinking about something for a second. Then, her final words were, 'Tell Brad that his friend with the big mustache is always watching.'"

Her face pleading for answers, Juanita looked at Brad. "Then she was just gone. She must have practically touched you as she left. I don't know, Brad. She simply vanished in the storm."

"Holy Jesus, Juanita. Holy Jesus."

"When she left, I was no more than three seconds behind her. And you say you never saw or heard anything."

"No, Juanita. I didn't see a thing. I had no idea that a person was in the shop with you." Brad hesitated. "If it was indeed a person."

Without speaking, Juanita and Brad sat quietly, hands interlocked. The ticking of the shop's clock now seemed loud, almost harsh. The sound of time's ceaseless march.

Becoming aware that the violent weather had abated and the storm had passed, Brad looked out the window. "Look, sweetheart, the sun is coming out. Let's go outside, get some fresh air, and let things settle in our minds."

With a nod, Juanita stood and stepped through the door. Brad followed. Once again seated, neither spoke. The cool breath of rain-cleansed mountains brushed their faces. Brad gazed into the branches of a nearby ponderosa pine. Lingering raindrops glistened like crystals in the sunlight. Adding to the wonderment of the moment, Brad watched in amazement as an owl perched in the tree and fluffed his wings. A soft hoot floated through the valley.

FIVE

The night seemed endless. The bewildering appearance of Juanita's visitor and her cryptic words were impossible to simply shrug off. Sleep would not come to their troubled minds. But neither Juanita or Brad were in a mood to discuss or attempt to analyze what had happened. Consumed with private thoughts, the night was spent within a largely silent embrace that held both love and disquiet. Breeze, stirring among trees, drifted through their opened window with the sound of a murmuring stream. Peace did not flow.

Giving up on sleep, Juanita and Brad rose soon after dawn. Mugs filled with freshy brewed coffee and yearning for the cold jolt of a mountain morning, they stepped outside. Hand in hand, they strolled the drowsy streets of Red River. They tasted the crispness of a new day as distinctly as the coffee. The morning warmed and sunlight lifted their spirits. Following a visit to their favorite bakery for more coffee and a taste of decadence, they found a bench only feet from the stream that was the namesake of the small village.

Seeking the tranquility that moving water offers for those who take time to listen, Juanita and Brad took the time. They listened. Quiet minutes passed. The lullaby worked its magic. Juanita finally spoke. "Tell me something. What is it about sunrises and sunsets that seems to bring about so much reflection within our minds? All through the night, I replayed the words of yesterday's visitor a thousand times. What was she trying to say about time not always moving forward? That woman's visit has caused me to think in a way that I've never done before. Does sunset mark the end of a day or the beginning of night? Just as much happens during night as happens during day, they are just different things. And why do we seem to view sunrise as a beginning rather than an end to a star-filled night?"

Juanita looked to Brad with a sly smile and an elbow jab to his ribs. "Sometimes night delivers the very best part of our lives. You agree?" Without giving Brad a chance to respond, Juanita continued. "I don't know how to take her words, but my visitor sure made me think. Is time something that is real or is it merely an illusion? Who is to say time can only move in a single direction? What kind of time transport took you to a cabin from a world long past where a woman, who apparently was me, cared for you and your injuries? Which way is time moving when we find ourselves together, absolutely certain that in another time, in another place, we knew each other?" Juanita was quiet, not really expecting a response.

The water of Red River flowed, always moving, always changing. Juanita and Brad sat, contemplating the mystery. Was the water of Red River running away from the past or rushing toward an unknown future?

Rising from the bench, Brad gave his torso a few twists before reaching for his toes in a badly needed stretch. "My brain is too old and too rusted to spend any more time worrying about this. I am thinking all of the things you are thinking, but I'm getting absolutely nowhere." With a breath of frustration, Brad paused. "I need to take a break, Juanita. Let my mind clear a bit." Stooping to the ground for a stone, he made a toss into the stream. "All I know for certain this morning is that I love you. Whether that love comes from another world or from that magical evening we spent beneath a windmill on your parent's ranch, I don't really care. For the moment, that's good enough for me. I have no interest in analyzing beyond that."

Juanita nodded that she understood but did not speak.

"Please call your prosecutor friend in Albuquerque." With a sarcastic grin, Brad continued. "You should probably handle that first thing this morning. I happen to sleep with a prosecutor from time to time. I know for a fact that those lawyer types have a tendency to get all wrapped up in meetings and legal nonsense. It will be good to know if your friend has any ideas about the guy who brought that pottery into your uncle's shop." Brad tossed another stone. "Give her a jingle while I take a stroll upstream for some serious exploring. Who knows, I may spot a secret hiding place for a trout that would be worth a visit with my rod." With a wave of his hand, Brad sauntered off, his eyes in search of promising riffles or pools.

———

By the time Brad returned from his walk, the sun had risen to a height that caused sparkles to dance across the water of Red River. Sounds of people and automobiles beginning a new day filled the streets. Brad smiled as he neared the bench where he had left Juanita. Her laugh always delivered a contagious sense of happiness and that was what he now heard. Following the somber hours since yesterday afternoon, lighthearted notes were especially appreciated.

Juanita was obviously concluding the conversation with her prosecutor friend with a bit of humorous banter. Lifting a finger to indicate that her talk was almost finished, Juanita punctuated her laughter with a wink and motioned for Brad to take a seat.

Placing her cell phone in her lap as she concluded her call, Juanita turned to look at Brad. "I have stuff to tell you, but first, I have to say that my talk with the office was a reminder of how much I have loved our time here. I was talking with Janice Weathers, the lady we have dinner with every so often. She always gives you grief about all the time and money you spend trying to catch a trout."

"Yeah, I remember Janice. I think I like her in spite of her smart-ass ways."

"In addition to being a ton of fun, Janice is a tremendous attorney. We bounce stuff off each other all the time. I value her friendship beyond words." Juanita paused to take a deep breath. "We laughed some, but we also talked some serious talk. We agree that we love what we do, but sometimes it seems we are trapped in an endless circle of the same stuff. Hearings, motions, jury selections, all-night trial prep. And then, it simply starts again. We live within an endless milieu of bureaucracy, crime, and criminals. And of course, victims are the common denominator in everything we do."

"I know exactly what you mean. It is sad but true that all too often criminals or their trials receive all the attention. Victims sometimes end up on the bottom of the heap."

"Remember that trial I had a couple of months ago that caused me to become so terribly upset? I'm talking about the one where a pregnant woman was killed by the bank robber who was a repeat offender. Her husband and other children were in my office during trial prep." Juanita became quiet. "It's seeing the faces and hearing the voices of the victims that's so difficult. I feel the weight of a shattered life on my shoulders every time I step into the courtroom to begin a trial." Juanita gazed into Red River, contemplating the rippling water. "For some reason, that weight has become terribly heavy in recent weeks."

Turning her head to look directly into Brad's eyes, Juanita spoke with intensity in her voice. "I mean it, Brad. The days in the gift shop with Uncle Foster have really impacted me. What is actually important in this life? And after yesterday's encounter with myself, or whoever the heck walked through that door, I think I need to be giving a lot more thought to this. Somebody way beyond me is talking. Somebody way beyond you and me both." She turned again to the water. "I think both of us need to be paying very close attention and think about the things that have happened to us."

Juanita did not say anything more as she continued staring into the river. Brad placed his hand over hers and joined her silence.

"Okay, so much for life's musings 101." Juanita broke the moment, releasing a sigh before speaking. "Let me tell you what Janice had to say about the mystery man and his pottery. I'm afraid she wasn't much help. The cases that she has dealt with have been primarily about people who go onto either public or private lands to plunder or steal protected artifacts. Simple as that." Juanita shrugged. "She agreed that the guy in Uncle Foster's shop sounds screwy but that's about it."

"Okay, pretty much what we expected, but thanks for trying."

"It was fun to catch up with the latest happenings in our office. But there was one more thing we talked about that is going to really upset you. I told Janice about what happened with the deer on Uncle Ernie's ranch. She told me that there is an open investigation down in southern New Mexico, somewhere in the Gila Wilderness, that involves the killing of a federal park ranger. Janice has the case for our office since it involves murder of a federal agent on federal land. Apparently, the poor guy was working alone when he surprised some poachers spotlighting game at night. He radioed to his headquarters what he had found. Apparently, he approached the people and was murdered. Murdered with an arrow, if you can imagine that. Shot right through his throat."

"Good Lord Almighty!"

Nodding her head, Juanita continued. "The arrow was removed from the ranger, but his body was left lying right where he fell. The crime scene appeared to have been hurriedly cleaned up. They are sure that more than one person was at the site when the ranger made his confrontation. Apparently, the poachers, accidentally left an arrow behind that was found partially buried beneath some leaves where they were conducting their hunt. It was some sort of high tech and very expensive arrow that is rather unusual. The investigators recovered a few partial fingerprints from the arrow shaft and some discarded beer cans but nothing adequate to conduct databank searches. If they develop a suspect and have a full set of prints to work with, they can probably make a good comparison."

"Jesus H." Brad looked upward to the sky.

"Yep. The ranger was a young guy with a family."

A despondent sigh was Brad's only response for several seconds. "A story like this makes you realize what could have happened if your Uncle Ernie's neighbor had been a couple of minutes earlier and surprised the guys poaching that poor buck."

A shudder rippled through Juanita's body as she nodded her agreement. "That is exactly what I thought about when Janice told me the story."

Juanita and Brad sat quietly, once again listening to the river. Finally, Brad spoke. "Thanks for calling Janice. I don't suppose we gained much but it was worth a try. I'm going to call the investigator out in Utah who arrested Luther Birdwell. Maybe he can shed some light on who this guy is and why he would show up in your uncle's shop."

"Sounds good. Go ahead with the call. I'm heading back to shower and get ready to open the shop." Juanita turned her head for a kiss before rising. "Thank you for a wonderful morning walk. The story about the ranger being murdered was a terrible way to begin our day. But outside of that, we needed this morning to recover from yesterday afternoon. See you in a bit." Flicking a wave over her shoulder, Juanita walked away.

———

Brad remained seated beside Red River to make his call to Utah. Following a self-introduction and a nutshell synopsis of his FBI career, Brad explained the reason for his call. Tucker Jenkins listened quietly as Brad related the story of the slaughtered deer near Flo and Ernie's ranch. Once Brad had concluded, Tucker's voice carried a tone of disgust. "I've been an investigator with the Utah Division of Wildlife Resources for a bunch of years and I've seen more stuff like you just described than you care to know. But the shock and repugnance will never fade. I get just as angry today as I did my first day on the job. Anything I can do to help, I will gladly do, but I'm in Utah and the story you just told me happened in New Mexico. Let me know how I can help and I'm on it."

"Well, I think there probably is a connection and that's why I'm calling you." Brad crossed his legs, getting more comfortable on the bench. "There is a second chapter to this story you need to hear. A close friend of mine, a police officer in Aspen, Colorado helped me out with a little research. According to arrest records that he pulled up, the next part of the story involves an old friend of yours."

"I like hearing about old friends. But I learned long ago that some old friends are better than other old friends. Since arrest records are involved, my gut tells me this is not going to be a good old friend."

Following a shared chuckle of understanding, Brad explained the strange visit that Juanita's uncle had received in his gift shop. After describing what had happened, Brad spoke deliberately. "Okay, this is the meat and potatoes of why I called you. When pressed to do so, this guy with the pottery very reluctantly produced a Utah driver's license. Does the name Luther Birdwell mean anything to you?"

A moment of loud silence hung before Tucker replied. "Are you serious? Luther Birdwell. Hell yes, his name means something to me! I arrested him a few years ago. He is a poacher to his core. The bastard slaughters animals for money, but I think it goes deeper than making a profit or greed. I honestly think the asshole has a perverted sense of enjoyment in cruelty or killing." Tucker paused. "And I can tell you that his perversion is not limited to animals. He thinks no more of human life than he does of a rodent. Luther Birdwell is one dangerous man."

"Wow! I'm aware of the computer info on his conviction and penalty in Utah. But it sounds like there is more to Luther than what the computer tells."

"I can sure as hell promise you that the computer tells only part of the story. What is not in some sanitized computer report is how that rotten bastard came within an inch of murdering me during his arrest."

"Uh-oh. This sounds serious."

"Serious as a forest fire. The investigation and arrest of Luther Birdwell could fill a book. In all my years of handling crimes involving violations of wildlife and game laws, the Birdwell case is the one that stands out as number one. And take my word, I've seen some crazy and foul stuff in my years."

"That's quite a statement."

"You bet it is. The case involved other states and several jurisdictions. After months of gathering evidence and interviewing dozens of both witnesses and accomplices, we developed several prosecutable cases. Everyone agreed that the most convincing evidence was here in Utah, so the big ticket ended up in my lap. Once our arrest and search warrants were signed, sealed, and delivered, we set up a plan and a day for his arrest. Of course, Murphy's Law kicked in at the last minute. The county sheriff's office made an emergency call for help just as we were heading out to grab Birdwell and search his place. A badly wanted arsonist out of California had been located in our territory. The sheriff's investigators were desperate for help to snag his ass and do a search of his motel room and vehicle."

Tucker Jenkins paused and Brad could hear his deep breath. "Admitting mistakes is never easy but I can't deny that I made a poor decision on that morning. My backup team for the Birdwell arrest had to leave to help grab the arsonist and handle that search warrant. I made a call that I would go ahead as planned but without backup." Tucker again stopped talking for a moment. "I'm here today to tell you this story, but only by the grace of the good Lord."

"You have my undivided attention. This is going to be one of those stories."

"Indeed, it is one of those stories. Like the saying goes, always better to be lucky than good. I was lucky as hell but somebody else was mighty good. My partner that morning was a lady named Lori Carpenter. She is drop-dead beautiful, one tough cookie, and a hell of a wildlife officer." Another deep breath came as Jenkins gathered his thoughts. "As usual, our arrest was planned for early in the morning, right at first light. Birdwell was living in a cabin that was way back in the woods and hard to approach. Because we wanted to surprise him, both for the arrest and to serve the search warrant, we parked our vehicle a good distance away. After sneaking through the forest, we reached the clearing where Birdwell's cabin was located. Lori circled way around to approach from the rear. I waited until she gave her radio signal that she was in place. I then stepped into the clearing and began walking toward the cabin. Lori did the same in the rear. The plan was for me to announce our presence at the front and Lori would be ready in case he did a jack rabbit out the back."

"My heart is pounding just listening to your story. Been there a hundred times."

"Yeah, my heart was pounding for sure. But I still had my head up my ass for even considering taking Birdwell on without more help. To this day, Lori can't describe exactly what happened, but she credits her guardian angel. While approaching the back door of the cabin, she simply sensed something bad wrong. Lori made a split-second decision to forget about covering the back door. She pulled her weapon and bolted around the cabin to the front. What she saw was ice-cold evil. Luther Birdwell was crouched down behind a rocker on his front porch. He had a crossbow and arrow, ready to fire. His aim was on me and his intention was to kill me dead."

"Jesus Christ!"

"Lori screamed bloody murder to distract him and drew down on his ass. It happened in a fraction of a second." Jenkins again paused. "Lori says that she will never forget the look on Birdwell's face as he slowly lowered his bow and stared straight into her face. She said the hatred in his eyes was chilling. His face and eyes haunt her to this day. If Lori had been one blink later in her decision to run to the cabin's front, I would not be here today to tell you this story."

"What a frigging story."

"Since it was only the two of us, we had no way to immediately transport his rotten balls off to jail. So, we basically hogtied his ass. We kept him secured where we could keep our eyes on him while we searched his cabin. That search was every bit as sickening as his intention to murder me. I stayed right beside the shitbird while Lori did the search throughout the cabin and in the front and rear areas. When it was all over, we had scrapbooks filled with photos of trapped animals, photos of lions and bobcats with maimed paws or shots to the gut with small caliber rounds. We found a bucket load of medicines to make animals groggy so they would be easy to track. Every kind of trap known to man was in his inventory."

"God almighty. You were dealing with one sick bastard."

"It was a chamber of horrors. But on top of all that stuff, he had kept newspaper articles where law enforcement reported poaching violations and extended a plea to the public asking for help. It was a classic case of a demented mind collecting trophies."

"This is as sick as anything I've ever heard." Brad spat his words.

"Yep, for sure. But I have to tell you. I watched Birdwell's face while Lori was conducting her search. That bastard's eyes never left her the whole time. Hatred radiated every second she moved about. He knew damned well that she was gathering evidence to send his ass away."

"I can only imagine."

Tucker Jenkins snorted. "I'm not sure if it was more frightening or satisfying when a few weeks later Birdwell went on trial. Lori was the principal witness, and man-oh-man, did she ever do a marvelous job. The jury was absolutely mesmerized by a talented, professional woman articulating a tale of such repugnance. From the moment she was sworn in, Birdwell's ship took on water and began to sink. Lori introduced the evidence she had obtained during the search of his cabin. And believe me, it was powerful stuff. One by one she produced the photographs of animals that had been wounded or maimed. Next were the medicines and tranquilizers. Then came all the journals and articles that Birdwell kept for bragging rights. I'm telling you, the jury hardly breathed during her testimony."

Brad took a moment to interject a comment. "I've never met this Lori lady, but God love the woman."

"Yeah, she definitely delivered for the good guys." Tucker Jenkins laughed. "In fact, our office still refers to the trial as the courtroom crucifixion. When the judge asked the defense lawyer if he wanted to cross examine, the poor guy barely managed a faint little squeak that he had no questions."

"I'm surprised Birdwell took his case to trial. Sounds like you had a solid case. Was there any talk of a plea deal?"

"Oh, heck yes. His own lawyer begged him to plead. Birdwell is flat out one mean-ass son of a bitch. That bastard will never surrender or give up. He will always go down swinging."

"Some guys are like that. And they are the dangerous ones if they get cornered."

"Absofuckinglutely. I watched Birdwell like a hawk throughout

Lori's testimony. The hatred in that man put goosebumps on my skin. When it was all over, I warned Lori that I was worried about him seeking revenge in some way."

"Hell yes."

"If there is such a thing as a defense attorney with a conscience, that trial was one of the few times I've seen one do the right thing. After it was all over and Birdwell was convicted, his attorney pulled Lori and me aside. He told us that he had concerns about Birdwell's mental stability. He said he had never known a person with such hatred for women. The defense attorney clearly feared for Lori. He said that if Birdwell ever had an opportunity, there was no telling what he might do. He also said if his client was ever again confronted by law enforcement, they darned well better be careful."

"That's somber stuff, coming from his own attorney."

"Yes, it is for sure." With a sarcastic laugh, Tucker continued, "So, that's my history with Luther Birdwell. Just in case you haven't figured it out, we ain't exactly pen pals. I don't have reliable sources to keep me up on his current activities. I've heard rumors that he was hanging his hat down in southern Colorado but that was quite some time ago. I sure don't know anything about connections he might have in New Mexico."

"Man alive!" Brad leaned forward and rubbed his brow as he spoke. "I don't know what to think about Luther coming into the gift shop with a goofy story about pottery. But it strikes me as more than coincidence that he happens to be in the area at the same time as the blatant poaching of the buck I just told you about."

Anger simmered in Jenkins's voice. "I can damn sure tell you one thing. If Luther Birdwell is anywhere near wildlife, he will violate any and all gaming laws if it brings him a lousy dollar. His demented personality and repugnant methods were clear as a bell after our search and everything that came out in trial. The jury, and everyone in the courtroom, had no doubts that Birdwell, and other so-called outfitters he associated with, would do anything for a dollar. In season or out of season, baiting, spotlighting, you name it, Birdwell did it. Like I said, he would trap a bear or a mountain lion, then maim a paw. He would even gut shoot the poor animal so that some high-paying client could easily track it for a kill."

"I have no words. There are no words."

"I agree."

Brad held his thoughts for a moment. "However, talk about coincidence. I learned of something just this morning that may very well be relevant." Brad related the story of the murdered ranger in southern New Mexico. "It's my understanding that they have some partial prints from the crime scene. It's certainly worth a shot to give them Birdwell's info for a comparison with a full set of prints."

"Absolutely. That poor ranger's murder has Luther Birdwell's signature written all over it."

"I think so too. Just call the United States Attorney's Office in Albuquerque. Ask for Janice Weathers. She's a great lady and can point you in the right direction to reach the investigators handling the case."

"Fantastic, I'm on it. And, if I can help in any way with anything down there in New Mexico, give me a shout. There is nothing in the world that would make me happier than to hammer nails in a coffin to put that SOB away for a long time."

———

With the call to Tucker Jenkins completed, Brad remained on the streamside bench. He felt a need for more time of introspection. Intuition told him that the story he had heard from Jenkins was not going to end. Something more was going to happen in the saga of Luther Birdwell. Just knowing that Luther Birdwell had been in Uncle Foster's gift shop, had stood within feet of Juanita, caused a sick knot to swell in Brad's stomach.

Brad had contemplated spending the afternoon on a trout stream. Time with his fly rod had sounded like a good idea, but that now held no appeal. He had to tell Juanita about Luther Birdwell. Together, they needed to talk with Uncle Foster. What should he do with the pottery? Was he safe in the gift shop with a person like Birdwell involved?

Placing his hands over his face, Brad stared into darkness. He also needed time with Juanita to try and make sense of yesterday's visit and the words spoken by the mystical woman. What had she meant about discovering life among those no longer living? Why had she made a point of reminding Juanita that at the time Brad was assaulted, Mustache had stated it would be Manuel's sister to care for him? Who was Manuel?

Brad lowered his hands, and without realizing that he did so, slightly moved his head from side to side as he stared into the flow of Red River. The time had come. There could be no more poking his head into a sandpile. With a deep breath, Brad made a confession to himself. He had been living in denial, suppressing something that could no longer be suppressed. After yesterday, his cowardice was obvious. Within his mind, Brad reluctantly admitted that he had actually met Manuel. He had looked into Manuel's eyes. He had held Manuel's hand, spoken to him, and heard his voice.

Whether he felt guilt, shame, or regret, Brad wasn't certain. But denial of something simply because he could not explain it was no longer a luxury or an option. There was something in his past that could no longer be ignored. He had to face it. But how to face it was the question. He had an idea. He dreaded doing so, but Brad knew he must finally come clean with Juanita.

Brad stood and began a slow, thoughtful walk to the gift shop and Juanita.

# SIX

THE DAY HAD PASSED with only a few clouds developing. Afternoon's heat had subsided, allowing Juanita and Brad to comfortably stroll in evening's beauty. At times their hands clasped. At other times, a brush of shoulders was their contact. However, never did more than a few seconds pass until one of them made an unconscious move to ensure that their bodies touched. Walking a faint set of ruts that served as a seldom-used road, they followed the meanderings of a creek. Brad had become familiar with the area as it was part of Ernie's ranch. The creek had been a fishing destination since Juanita and he had begun their stay in Red River.

They moved in silence, each searching within their own minds for a way to make sense of all that they had been discussing. Brad had told Juanita about Luther Birdwell. They had talked again of Juanita's visitor of the previous day. They analyzed each word the woman had spoken and the tone with which she delivered her message.

The time had arrived. Brad was on the brink of making his dreaded confession to Juanita. He was ready to explain that he had allowed a fog of denial to obscure some things that he had experienced before they came together. He had to tell her that he had actually met the person named Manuel. He wanted to assure her that the fog was now gone and that it would not return. He struggled to compose words that would make sense. How could he say something that sounded so strange, even to himself? What could he say to her about what he knew must be done?

Brad opened his mouth to speak. The opportunity of the moment vanished in a blink.

As if by design, the creek and the road made a synchronized bend, departing from an area of open meadow into dense forest. Brad had parked their vehicle within this canopy of trees and brush an hour earlier to begin their walk. Now, just before reaching where they had left the truck, the solitude they had been enjoying all evening was broken by the throaty sound of an oncoming vehicle. A dark-colored pickup truck appeared, approaching from the next curve in the road. The pickup truck headed directly toward them but moved at an abnormally slow speed. The pickup completely halted for a moment as it reached Brad's parked truck. After a few moments, it continued with a creeping pace.

Without speaking, Juanita and Brad had identical simultaneous thoughts. Where had the pickup truck come from? In their long walk, no vehicles had passed them on the road which meant the vehicle must have been ahead of them when they began hiking. Since the road was on Ernie's private property, the questions of who and why were obvious. The pickup truck eased past Juanita and Brad as they were forced to step aside to allow passage. A look of alarm and surprise was clear on the driver's face as the pickup inched past. Upon passing, the pickup quickly accelerated and sped away.

Brad felt the grip of Juanita's hand tighten before she spoke. "Brad, that was the man who brought the pottery into Uncle Foster's shop. That was Luther Birdwell."

An intense look into Juanita's face was Brad's questioning reply.

"Brad, it was him. I'm absolutely certain!"

Silence continued to be Brad's response as he processed what was happening. He had just laid eyes on Luther Birdwell. What followed in his mind was logical conjecture. Luther Birdwell was alone, on private property, in early evening. Tucker Jenkins's description of

Luther Birdwell's criminal actions and personality returned in hair-raising detail. Brad's mind knew with certainty that Birdwell was poaching. What other reason could there be for his creeping along the road in such a slow and deliberate manner?

The knot in his stomach that he had felt earlier in the day began to roil. Luther Birdwell had been inside the shop, only feet away from Juanita. Now, he was back. His cold eyes had briefly glared at Brad, but they had primarily focused on Juanita.

Before Brad could gather his thoughts to speak, Juanita grabbed his arm and whispered, panic in her voice. "Oh my God, Brad, look." Extending her arm, Juanita pointed. The knot in Brad's stomach swelled with nausea. In the middle of the road, only a few feet from where Brad had parked his truck, a doe deer stood. Her body hunched in an abnormal twist, she was in obvious distress. The doe took a step and stopped, struggling to move. The gruesome image unfolding before their eyes seared like fire as Juanita dug her fingers into Brad's arm. The doe took another step, her entire body quivering. An arrow's shaft protruded from her left hip in a grisly torment.

The deer turned her head, instinctively sensing human presence. Juanita and Brad felt the heat of her gaze as she spotted them. Her agony apparent, the animal clearly feared that she faced additional threat, but her eyes also pled for mercy.

They remained silent and unmoving for seconds but what seemed like eternity. Juanita again pointed. Her voice hoarse, she whispered, "Look, Brad, just beyond our truck."

Brad forced his eyes to break the gaze he had held with the doe and looked to where Juanita pointed. A fawn, its body decorated with white spots, looked to the doe, bewilderment and fear in its eyes.

Rational thought struggled to take control within each of their minds. "What should we do?" Juanita's voice was hushed as if the injured doe might be listening.

"We have no choice but to move toward her. She is right beside our truck." A sense of helplessness settled over Brad as he spoke. "Once we move toward her, she is going to run. I have no idea what the fawn will do." Silence followed as Juanita and Brad contemplated their options, all of which were bad. "I can't tell if the arrow is deeply embedded in her hip," Brad said. "Even if it's only a superficial wound, I don't see how the arrow will ever come out on its own."

"She is going to endure a horrible, slow death, and the fawn will also die." Exasperation and heartbreak filled Juanita's words.

"I don't know what's best, but we can't just stand here till darkness." A muffled swear followed as Brad began a slow, deliberate approach toward the injured deer. Juanita fell into step as they both focused their eyes directly into the doe's terrified gaze. Step by step they advanced. As they approached, it became apparent that the creature's body quivered. Whether her trembling was from fear or agony, there was no way to know. Intuition acted as an unspoken command, bringing Juanita and Brad to a halt within a few feet of the doe. Fear, blended with pleading, was palpable in the deer's eyes. Her body heaved in desperate breathing as two humans stood dangerously close.

Seconds dragged with neither the deer, Juanita, nor Brad moving. Suddenly and without warning, the doe abruptly lurched from the roadway. Thrashing through a barrier of brush to the creek's edge, her desperation culminated in an airborne hurtle as she attempted to leap across the stream. The weakened hip failed to deliver its usual acrobatic strength. Her front legs landed in midstream, with her hind legs crashing into a tangled brush pile that clogged the steam's bank. In frantic thrashing, the deer struggled to right herself and flee, but a pathetic reality quickly became apparent. The doe's hind legs were hopelessly entangled between a fallen tree trunk and the stream's edge. The impaled arrow remained above water. As the deer labored, the shaft undulated in a gruesome grip of its prey.

Guttural sounds escaped from within the trapped deer's lungs. Her eyes rolled in terror.

Recognizing the predicament of the deer's entrapment, but also aware of the damage that could be delivered by flailing hooves, Brad made his decision. Handing his phone and truck keys to Juanita, he lowered his body into the water. The deer had fallen into a bend within the creek that held surprising depth. Brad sucked hard as icy water enveloped his chest. Once his feet were secure, he ran his hands beneath the deer's body, seeking a way to set her free. Brad's heart sank as the severity of her predicament became clear. Her back legs were tightly wedged between a large tree trunk that had lodged into the river's bend and shoreline. There was no way to lift her body in a manner that would free her legs. Making matters even worse, she was held in an awkward position that forced her head and shoulders to be lower than the rear of her body. Brad realized that if the doe became exhausted, holding her head above water would become an impossible task. She would surely drown while trapped.

Resisting panic, Brad forced himself to think. The tree trunk was way too large and heavy to be moved. The rear legs of the deer were pinched into the riverbank so tightly that Brad feared she could easily suffer broken bones as she struggled. He gasped and, feeling his heart pound within his chest, looked up to Juanita. Their eyes locked and spoke urgently. The deer's life hung in precarious balance with the decisions and actions that they would make in the next few seconds. Juanita moved her head from side to side to side. Hatred for the person responsible for this deed and the weight of the life-determining decision now required were communicated without words.

"Okay, Juanita, we can save this deer. But we are going to have to act quickly." Brad's voice carried more certainty than he felt. "Get in the truck and go for Uncle Ernie. There's no cell signal down here. We have to have the chainsaw that he carries in his trailer. We need him and his saw here as fast as possible." Brad heard a tremor in his own words. He did not know if it was from the cold water, fear, or simple rage.

Giving a nod and without speaking, Juanita ran. Brad heard the rumble of his truck's engine and the sound of tires spinning in acceleration. The murmur of moving water and frenzied bursts of breath from the wounded deer became Brad's only companions. He felt terribly alone.

Cautiously moving his feet over the creek's slippery bottom, Brad inched his way through the water, making a way toward the deer's head. Liquid brown eyes tracked his movement, terror, uncertainty, begging. Brad felt pain in his own heart. Keeping in mind the hooves that could deliver crippling damage, Brad kept well to the doe's side. Gradually, he maneuvered his body into a position where he felt safe from being kicked, but offered a clear field of vision from the eyes of the doe. He hoped that if she could see him more clearly, she may feel less threatened than if he remained behind her. With eyes locked, animal and human momentarily settled into a motionless stare. The deer evaluated a creature that she instinctively feared. Brad evaluated a creature that he instinctively loved.

Making certain that his eyes never left the doe's face, and holding his voice low, Brad spoke as if she could understand language. Words of comfort, encouragement, and sympathy came from his lips. He told her that help was on the way. If she could manage to hang on, she would soon be reunited with her fawn. He told her of his determination to find the man who had perpetrated this horrible deed upon her.

Brad questioned within his mind if he spoke to calm the deer or to calm himself. What difference did it make? He continued his dialog and held the doe's eyes with his.

With the intensity of his concentration on the deer, it took more time than it should have for Brad to become aware of the sounds of an approaching vehicle. A brief glimmer of hope surged that Juanita and Ernie were arriving. But the hope was short-lived. Brad knew the sound of his own vehicle and that was not what was coming toward him. He also knew the sound of a ranch pickup pulling a trailer. It was not Uncle Ernie's rig on the road. Brad recognized the deep engine rumble as the large, heavy-duty pickup truck that had earlier driven past Juanita and him.

Brad gulped air and held it. A threat was imminent. Luther Birdwell had returned.

The pickup came to a halt on the roadway above the creek. After a few seconds, the driver maneuvered into the dense brush that grew alongside the road. Brad recognized the reason for this as a means of concealment to other vehicles that might arrive. Heart thundering, Brad watched as Luther Birdwell remained seated in the pickup, both hands on the steering wheel. It was easy to see Birdwell's face and eyes as he scrutinized the scene. The vulnerable position Brad occupied was sickeningly obvious. Standing in chest-deep water, beside the wounded deer, he was completely defenseless.

The water in which Brad had been standing was taking a toll. A chill seeped through his body.

Birdwell continued to simply sit and stare at Brad and the deer. Shivers rippled as Brad shifted his feet over the creek's bottom, anticipating what he feared was about to unfold. With what seemed to Brad as exaggerated slowness, the pickup's door finally opened. Birdwell's focus on Brad never wavered as he twisted his body to swing his legs from the pickup and to the ground. Late afternoon sun reflected perfectly. The glimmer of a crossbow within Birdwell's hand was unmistakable. Birdwell stood erect before closing the vehicle's door with his free arm. The slamming door sounded like a gunshot.

With calculated steps, Birdwell moved across the road toward the creek's edge. From his elevated position, he towered over Brad as a Goliath looking down upon his prey. Slowly shaking his head, he glared down on Brad before finally speaking. "Some folks just don't have the good sense to mind their own damned business." Birdwell's voice was deep and he spoke slowly. "Why do you suppose that is?" Birdwell stood in silence as if he expected a response.

Brad's mind was spinning. Birdwell had seen Juanita when he passed them standing beside the road. Could he have recognized her from the gift shop? Had he seen her as she drove for help? Brad could not even fathom the obvious question. Had Birdwell managed to stop Juanita? The crossbow in Birdwell's hand shimmered with evil.

"I thought about not coming back, just letting you go. But knowing that the little lady you are with probably remembers me from that silly-ass gift shop." Birdwell moved his head in a sad gesture. "Letting you go was just not an option. I thought long and hard about it. Nope, no option."

Birdwell looked to the sky as if he searched for an answer to a great mystery. "I had to come back. I just can't let this go." Birdwell was quiet again as he contemplated his words. "Ain't life got a way of getting things all mixed up? Why the hell did the two of you have to come walking on this very road on this very night? I had no quarrel with you. No quarrel at all."

Turning his head, Birdwell spit. A glob of tobacco-stained muck splattered on the ground. Birdwell continued, his words coming in slow cadence. "But now, I got a quarrel with you. Yep, I got a big quarrel." Looking at the wounded deer, Birdwell was quiet for a moment before he continued. "The two of you could have gone walking in town somewhere, had yourselves a big ol' strawberry ice cream cone and talked nice and friendly with folks out on the street." He hesitated as he pointed to the deer. "Now this." Another shake of his head. "I saw that little lady of yours driving like hell for help. So, when she comes back, and whoever comes with her, well, I suppose I'll have to quarrel with them too."

Silence hung heavy in the air, broken only by the sound of moving water and short breaths emanating from both Brad and the deer. "Too damned much quarreling for my liking. But you and your little lady give me no choice." Birdwell shifted his gaze to the deer. "And all for a damned little pissant deer."

In spite of his fear, Brad recognized the significance of what he had just heard. Juanita was safe, at least for now.

Birdwell's face became contemplative in moments of silence. "I recently met another person that got mixed up in life's complications. Why did he have to drive down the road, in the middle of the night, just as I happened to have a deer in my spotlight. Another pissant deer and another person not knowing when to just keep on truckin' and leave well enough alone." Birdwell appeared to be thinking as he twisted his head for another spit. "I had to quarrel with that man just like I reckon I now got to quarrel with you." Birdwell lifted the crossbow into the crook of his arm. Giving a nod to the weapon as he stroked the bow as if it were a pet, he again spoke. "This here is how I settle my quarrels. It ain't exactly the best way to settle matters, but like I said, life has a way of getting things all mixed up. I'm sorry for our quarrel, mister. You just should not have taken this particular road on this particular evening." Arms and hands moved in a flash of rehearsed precision. Brad sucked a breath. The crossbow was poised and aimed.

Diving, Brad sought the only cover he had. He held his body beneath the trunk of the fallen tree that had trapped the deer. Frantically trying to think of some means of escape or a strategy to fight, Brad remained submerged beneath the tree trunk. His lungs on fire, there was no escape. A breath and another dive was all he could do. Keeping his head as close to the tree trunk as possible, Brad exposed himself for a desperately needed gasp. He surfaced, eyes open and on Birdwell. He saw, heard and felt the arrow slam into the tree trunk, inches from his face. A rush of displaced air from the missed shot blew across his forehead. Brad inhaled, sucking with all his strength. Did he have time for one more gasp? There was no choice, he had to breathe.

With unfathomable speed, Birdwell reloaded a new arrow into the crossbow. Desperately risking a last gulp of air, Brad saw the loaded crossbow level directly into his face. Time mutated. A sequence of slow-motion events materialized, cold clarity in their imagery: an arrow's tip, razored blades. A smile twisting Birdwell's lips into an upward slant. The thumping of Brad's heart, spewing final burst of life. Time returned. The mad screeching of an owl echoed over the creek. Flying directly into Birdwell's face, thundering wings held the bird in place as talons ripped flesh and, with devastating efficiency, shredded soft eye tissue.

Wrapping his arms over the tree trunk for support, Brad watched the scene before him in stunned disbelief. Luther Birdwell was on his back, prone and screaming. His entire body convulsed as arms and hands thrashed at his attacker. As quickly as it had appeared, and with a final screech, the bird spread its wings and disappeared. Through his dazed state, Brad recognized opportunity. Summoning a strength he did not feel, he hoisted his body out of the water and onto the tree trunk. Arms extended and hands clawing into the soil of the river's edge, he dragged his legs over the tree to pull himself onto the bank. Lying on his belly, chest heaving, Brad tried to clear his mind. He watched as Birdwell raised his body into a sitting position, hands covering his face and eyes. Brad spotted the crossbow lying in the grass, several feet away. He surmised that Birdwell had flung it away when the owl attacked. As Brad surveyed the scene, the reassuring sounds of Uncle Ernie's truck and trailer became clear. He saw Juanita and Ernie pull to a stop on the road. He realized that they were not aware of Luther Birdwell's pickup that was concealed in brush. They had no idea of what was happening.

Birdwell also heard the arrival. He lowered his hands and looked toward Brad. Mangled flesh, blood, and other fluids flowed, saturating his face. Birdwell leapt to his feet and, with a curdling scream, bolted across the road to his pickup.

Having no idea of what was happening, Juanita and Uncle Ernie stared in amazement as they witnessed a crazed and bloodied man half stagger and half sprint across the road. They watched in stupefied silence as Birdwell made it to his pickup. In a whirl of spewing dust and gravel, the vehicle spun in a turn and was gone before their eyes and minds even began to process what was happening.

As Birdwell and his pickup truck disappeared, Juanita and Ernie turned to face the creek. Juanita screamed.

Now on all fours, Brad lifted an arm to indicate that he was all right. Juanita and Ernie were by his side in a blink. Ernie's eyes narrowed into slits while Juanita's became oversized ovals as the significance of the scene registered. Brad was drenched, face covered with mud. Water within his lungs rattled each breath. A crossbow lay on the ground and, most nightmarish of all, the shaft of an arrow protruded from the tree trunk at the water's edge.

Kneeling beside Brad, Juanita placed her arms about his shoulders. Pressing her body as close as possible, her voice somewhere between a sob and a scream. "Oh my God! Oh my God!"

Coughing water in gasps, mucus dripped from Brad's mouth. He shook his head before speaking, "I'm okay, Juanita. I promise, I'm okay."

Ernie remained standing near Brad's head, maintaining a stoic silence. When Brad looked up, Ernie extended a hand. "Grab ahold."

Accepting the offer, Brad stood and felt strength and balance returning. Words did not seem appropriate for the moment, and no one spoke. As Juanita stood, she fell into Brad's embrace, their bodies swaying in the significance of the moment.

Brad finally broke the silence. Releasing Juanita and turning to the creek and the deer, he spoke softly. "I'll tell you everything that happened, but this poor thing can't last much longer. Let's set her free and then we can talk."

Looking around at his surroundings, Brad spoke. "Don't touch that arrow or crossbow. We'll cut the tree trunk. Leave the arrow in it just as it is." He turned to Juanita. "While Uncle Ernie gets his chain saw, you need to photograph the arrow and the crossbow. Get a shot of everything that you see around us. We'll take it all to a lab in Santa Fe tomorrow."

Muttering softly, Ernie spoke for the first time. "Son of a bitch. Son of a Goddamned bitch." Turning sharply, he sprinted to his trailer. Juanita nodded her understanding, pulled her cell phone from her pocket, and began photographing.

"Here's the saw and I brought this also." Assuming command, Ernie lifted a container into the air and spoke with authority. "This is a powerful antibiotic that I use on my cows. Doc Truman says it's the best." Ernie looked at the arrow protruding from the doe's hip. "I have no idea how hard it's going to be, but we're gonna have to pull that arrow out of her. If it's lodged in bone, it won't be easy and she's going to hurt like the devil."

Ernie looked to Juanita who had completed taking photographs. "We're going to have to pull the arrow while she's still trapped. Once she's free, she will sure as hell run. When the arrow comes out, I need you to pour this antibiotic right into the wound."

"I'm ready, Uncle Ernie." Juanita took the container, dropped to her knees, and positioned herself at the water's edge so that she could reach the deer's hip.

Brad thought for a moment. "I have no idea what to expect once you start pulling on that arrow. I sure as hell don't know what she will do when you fire up the saw. I'm afraid that if she goes crazy, she might break one or both of her trapped legs. I'm going to get back in the water, stand beside her and hopefully steady her while you do what you have to do. Whether I'll be a distraction or a comfort, I don't know, but it's the best thing I can think of."

With a sharp nod of agreement, Ernie's voice was curt. "Okay, folks, let's do it."

Brad eased his body back into the creek and shuffled through the water until he once again stood close the doe's head. "Hey, little lady, I'm back with you." His voice soft and steady, Brad tried to engage her eyes. "We're going to get you out of here. Your baby is waiting. This will soon be all be over." Brad gulped a breath and his heart thundered. The doe's eyes bulged, liquid moons of brown, brimming with terror. Brad looked to Juanita and then to Ernie. With a desperate breath, Brad gave his head a nod.

On his knees at the water's edge, Ernie was able to extend his arm to reach the impaled arrow. He lowered his head and whispered, "Dear God, help us please. And show your mercy to this poor creature." Raising his head, Ernie's next words were spoken with military precision. "Here's what I'm going to do. I'll grab the arrow right where it entered her body and give it a couple of hard rocks back and forth. Then I'm going to pull straight up with everything I have." Ernie paused. "Pray like hell this damned thing comes out." Ernie looked to Brad. Brad nodded his understanding. Ernie looked to Juanita. Her eyes acknowledged what was going to happen.

A hard inhale. Leathered skin, calloused palms and Ernie's powerful fingers grasped the arrow shaft. Forward-back, side-to-side. The deer screamed. Juanita screamed. Brad closed his eyes, unable to watch. Ernie's arm pulled straight up in a vicious wrench. He lifted it high. The entire arrow, bloodied tip and all, in his grasp. Juanita leaned over the water to reach the doe's hip. Pouring brown liquid from the container, she filled the grisly cavity left in the wake of the removed arrow.

Brad didn't know if animals experienced shock in the same manner as humans, but he felt the doe was either on the verge of unconsciousness or total exhaustion. Her chest heaved in labored breath. Her eyes were now glazed, not seeming to register anything happening around her. Juanita, Ernie, and Brad exchanged looks, each gasping, whispering a prayer of gratitude for the first victory but realizing the battle was not yet won.

Ernie reached for the chain saw. Flipping the ignition switch, he adjusted the choke and gave a yank on the starting rope. A cough and a burst of smoke. Another pull. The engine sputtered. "Come on, you son of a bitch." A violent pull on the rope. The engine caught, coughed, and finally growled. Ernie's finger pumping on the gas trigger, the engine finally began to roar. Bending into the tree trunk, Ernie lowered the screaming chain to meet the wood. Using her bare hands, Juanita held back smaller branches to give the saw clear access. Smoke, sawdust, the smell of burning oil. Ernie put his weight into the saw. The chainsaw howled. Heat rose. Sparks flew when striking bits of gravel embedded in the bark.

The saw's roar reignited the deer's panic. Her eyes again bulged. She began flailing her front legs, and Brad could only guess at the stress she was placing on her trapped rear legs. Ignoring his fear of what her hooves could do, Brad adjusted his body until he was able to place his arms about the deer's neck. Wedging his feet into the creek's bottom, he held her body with all of his strength. If he could prevent her from lunging, perhaps she would not break her back legs.

With the deer's neck held between his shoulder and cheek, Brad was unable to monitor the progress of Ernie's saw. He held his breath when Ernie's voice shouted, "First cut finished. Second cut beginning."

Tremors racked the doe's body, but she did not lunge. Ernie and Juanita worked together. The saw slowed and quieted. Ernie shouted a warning. "We're almost through. Be ready. When the tree cuts loose, as long as she hasn't broken a leg, she's gonna run."

"Ready!"

The saw again bellowed. Brad felt the release of pressure as the severed tree trunk lost its grip on the deer's legs. He released the deer's neck and shoved his body away. Brad's feet slipped on the creek's bottom, causing him to fall. Totally submerged once again, Brad felt no panic. This time, some crazy bastard wasn't waiting at the surface wanting to kill him. Brad found his footing and lifted his head above the surface. With a gulp of air, he looked around. The doe was standing on the opposite side of the creek. In a moment of confusion, or possibility gratitude, she remained still as she looked back to the people and to the place where she had almost lost her life. She moved with a limp, but in a moment, the doe disappeared into the forest.

Evening's long shadows fell across the stream in a tapestry of water, light and sky. Brad waded the creek to its bank. Juanita and Ernie each extended a hand to help him up onto solid ground.

After the arrow that had been removed from the doe and the crossbow were loaded into the back of Ernie's vehicle, the tree trunk, with its embedded arrow, was left lying on the ground. Juanita, Ernie, and Brad stood together. Thoughts of what had almost happened prevented anyone from speaking. Upon an unspoken command, Ernie and Brad bent to hoist the tree trunk into the vehicle. Juanita covered everything with a blanket. A somber silence became their bond as the final light of evening settled. A surreal sensation that the past minutes had taken them to a world somewhere between a dream and reality was unspoken. No one wanted to break the silence.

Keeping with the moment, Juanita did not utter a sound as she pointed toward the forest. The doe and her fawn stood together.

# SEVEN

Conversation was unnecessary. They had said all there was to say. Upon returning home from the wounded deer and their encounter with Luther Birdwell, Juanita had called Janice Weathers to explain what had happened. Recognizing the significance of what she heard, and the probable connection to the murder of the ranger in southern New Mexico, Janice promised to have the appropriate investigators in Santa Fe the following morning. The tree trunk, arrows, and crossbow were transferred to Brad's truck for transport to Santa Fe and laboratory analysis. Juanita and Brad then collapsed into bed.

Their night had passed in fierce embrace, broken by spasms of raw emotion. Words of what they had seen and felt were spoken. Tears of anger and hatred were torrid. Tears of relief were shed in passion. Morning's light was slow to come.

---

Music from the truck's radio and passing scenery were the desired companions as Juanita and Brad passed through Taos and continued to Santa Fe. Brad drove while Juanita reclined her seat. Her hand over Brad's, she allowed herself to become lost in the quiet and gentle swaying of the vehicle. From time to time, Juanita closed her eyes, but she did not close them in rest. The brief moments of darkness served only to illuminate what lay in the truck's cargo area. Behind her sealed eyelids, Juanita saw a crossbow and an arrow with a blood-crusted tip. Most clearly seen with her imposed blindness was a tree trunk with an embedded arrow. The arrow had come within a whisper of murdering the man whose hand she now held. With deliberate effort, she kept her eyes opened. She preferred not to see.

Heading south on Highway 68, Juanita and Brad cruised along the banks of the Rio Grande. When they passed the road leading to La Chiripada Winery, without speaking, they each cherished memories of when they had together explored the enchanted vineyards of this secluded slice of paradise. That day had held pure happiness as they strolled vineyards and sipped wine. It now felt like something from a past life. A life before Luther Birdwell. A life before a visitor from mystic origins. Part of another world and another time.

After clearing the sprawl of Española, Brad broke their silence. Pointing to the east, he spoke more to himself than to Juanita. "I know a man who once lived here, on the Nambe Pueblo Reservation. He is now a famous artist. I'm going to reach out to him as soon as we get this business in Santa Fe handled. I think he can help us understand a few things."

With a lazy nod of acknowledgment, Juanita spoke softly. "Whatever you say. I can't think about anything else right now."

Once again lost in their own thoughts, Juanita and Brad drove without talking. Visions of yesterday's nightmare were impossible to erase.

———

Standing in stark contrast to the gentle adobe architecture that symbolizes Santa Fe, the New Mexico Department of Public Safety office building appeared as a fortress. Rectangular walls dotted with elongated, rectangular windows, imposed an air of harsh formality. A United States flag undulated in the late morning breeze. The flag of New Mexico flew beneath. Brilliant yellow and bearing the red sun symbol of the Zia People, the flag was captivating against the brilliant blue of morning's sky. Representing the four seasons, the four directions, and the four stages of life, Brad felt the flag to be the most welcoming feature of the building.

While waiting in the parking lot, Juanita punched numbers into her cell phone. Janice Weathers answered on the second ring. Janice had taken control and notified the investigator handling the murder of the ranger in southern New Mexico, along with the Albuquerque FBI agent assigned to the case. They had all driven to Santa Fe the previous evening in preparation for meeting with Juanita and Brad.

Janice and the team exited the building and began walking toward Brad's truck. Juanita hurriedly exited the vehicle and was the first to meet Janice. Before any words were exchanged, they embraced. Awkward silence held while the women, who had been friends for years, had their moment. The trauma of the previous evening permeated. A sense of solemnity held as introductions were finally made.

Placing an arm about Juanita's shoulder and holding her close, Brad spoke. "Thank you all for making this trip on short notice. We had quite an evening yesterday. But now that it's all over and we are fine, I feel pretty certain that some good is going to come out of this." Brad directed his words to the investigator handling the murder of the ranger.

Turning to Janice and the FBI agent, Brad continued. "Janice, thank you so much for stepping up and making this happen. Juanita and I were pretty washed out last night. I understand that you have the case for the prosecutor's office and the Bureau is involved since a federal agent was murdered on federal land. But I'm an outsider now. I would not know who to call."

A murmur of acknowledgment rippled through the group. The investigator for the New Mexico Department of Game and Fish,

Charles Carson, followed Brad's words. "Believe me, we are all happy that you are here to meet with us today. We've been talking this morning, and we agree that your close call may very well turn out to be the break we've been praying for. We are ready to go to work."

The FBI agent, Glenn Snyder, spoke next. "I've heard about you," he said looking to Brad. "But you can be certain that our entire Albuquerque office absolutely loves working with this lady here." Snyder smiled and nodded to Juanita. "When we are filing a case or need solid legal advice, we line up outside Juanita Ferris's office and wait our turn."

"I'll pay you later for that compliment." Juanita's laugh was tinged with both gratitude and embarrassment.

Opening the rear area of his truck, Brad's tone became all business. "What's first here, folks? I'm thinking the physical evidence from yesterday is the most critical."

Janice, Charles, and Glenn were obviously moved as they looked at the arrow that had been removed from the doe, the arrow that remained embedded within a tree log, and the crossbow. The lethal power of the weapons, along with a realization of what they had almost done, and what they had probably done to a ranger, cast a sobering aura over the group.

Juanita turned away, refusing to look.

Charles Carson stepped closer for a better look. "Lab techs are on the way right now. They will take this straight to the state laboratory for expedited examination." Carson squinted and bent his body over the blood-crusted arrow that had been removed from the wounded deer. "I can sure as hell tell you that this arrow looks to be exactly like the one we found at the murder scene of our ranger." A grave expression shadowed his eyes as he straightened. "It's a call for the scientists, but you can go to the bank that the shaft and the tip are twins to what we recovered."

Janice followed Carson's observation with authority. "If the lab can confirm that, with even a partial match of fingerprints, I'll have the paperwork ready for a warrant faster than you can count to three." She inhaled. "This makes me sick."

Directing his question to the group, Brad asked, "Have you

spoken with a guy named Tucker Jenkins? He's a game ranger out in Utah who had a close shave with Birdwell almost nailing him with a crossbow."

Snyder and Carson shook their heads simultaneously. "Oh yeah," Snyder replied. "We were on the phone with him yesterday and again this morning. He wants Birdwell to go down so bad he can taste it. I promise you, he won't be leaving his phone for a second until he hears from us."

A blue van with no windows pulled up beside the gathered group. A man and woman stepped out, both obviously acquainted with Charles Carson. After a brief round of introductions, Carson pointed to the items in Brad's truck. "This is it. This is what we have. The ball is in your court. You have my reports, and you know all about this Birdwell character that we're looking at." Carson placed his hands beneath his chin in a prayerful gesture. "We will be standing by. Work your magic with microscopes and test tubes. Do what you gotta do."

Papers requiring signatures to certify chain of custody were quickly signed and the lab techs departed with their macabre cargo.

Janice reached for Juanita's hand and began to lead the group. "Follow me, everyone. We need to take your statements and then you can be on your way." Janice and Juanita quietly whispered to one another as they walked. The men gave them respectful distance, understanding the intimate bond obviously shared by the veteran prosecutors walking in front of them.

Once inside and following offers of food or drink, it was decided that Juanita would provide her statement in writing. Because of the life-threatening actions taken by Luther Birdwell, and the potential for attempted murder charges to be filed in the future, Brad was asked to provide his statement by means of oral interview. He readily agreed.

Juanita was given access to a computer in a private room where she could prepare her statement. While Juanita handled this aspect of the day's proceedings, the investigative team gave Brad a synopsis of the ranger's murder and details of the crime scene search. Once Juanita had completed her statement, they stepped into a conference room that held adequate seating for all. Seats were taken in preparation and a recording device was centrally placed. Juanita took a seat at the back of the room, removed from the group. Brad noticed that she deliberately positioned her body so that she looked away from him.

The opening formalities and legal requirements of the interview were handled by Janice Weathers. Following introductory remarks and questions, Brad was mostly left alone to relate his story as he chose to tell it. From time to time, a member of the team would interject with a point of clarification, but interruptions were few. The recording device performed its duties in silence.

Janice Weathers, Charles Carson, and Glenn Snyder appeared to be hypnotized as Brad told his story. Pens and note pads were forgotten. Brad walked them through the gruesome details of the wounded deer. Following this part of the story, Brad related his encounter with Luther Birdwell in minute detail. He described the tone of voice used by Birdwell and articulated his facial expressions and body language. Without shame, Brad told of the fear that he had felt with an arrow tip aimed directly into his face.

Giving total concentration to his statement, Brad had failed to keep an eye on Juanita. As he told of his thoughts when the crossbow was inches from his face, and he had helplessly waited to feel the impact of an arrow into his skull, Brad abruptly ceased speaking. His eyes focused on Juanita, who had completely turned her back to him. As she leaned forward, her face buried in her hands, Brad's heart shattered. Trembling rippled across Juanita's shoulders.

Puzzled by Brad's abrupt change in demeanor, it took a few seconds for the interviewing team to recognize the abrupt alteration in Brad's eyes. It was apparent that his attention had shifted to Juanita. The remaining people in the room had ceased to exist in Brad's mind. Comprehension of the lack of sensitivity they had demonstrated hit the group like an invisible fist to the gut. For them, the interview had been clinical. It was an analysis of events or evidence to further an investigation. They were simply following a means to obtain an arrest warrant and develop a prosecutable case.

The process was personal and soul-wrenching trauma for Juanita.

A veil of embarrassment and shame descended upon the room. Janice rose from her seat. Grabbing a water bottle and a box of tissues, she approached softly. Placing her offering onto Juanita's lap, she lay a hand on her shoulder and applied gentle pressure.

A whispered "Thank you" was heard as Juanita reached for a tissue.

"I think we all need a break. Let's take five and then wrap this up." Janice spoke firmly, but recognizing her own failure and the group's blunder, reticence tinged her voice.

Uncomfortable nods and a shuffling of feet and bodies followed. Janice turned the recording device off and the team wandered out of the room. Brad bolted to Juanita. Their embrace was silent and intense.

"I am so sorry. I am so very sorry." Brad choked on his words as he spoke softly. "You should not have even been in the room for this."

Breaking the embrace, Juanita reached for a tissue to clear her eyes and nose. "No, that's not correct at all, Brad. You had given me a sanitized version of what happened in that creek. I heard it all last night. I thought I had processed it. I thought I was ready." Juanita shivered as she was quiet for a moment. "But I was nowhere near prepared to hear your story in such detail. Maybe I've been in denial. I don't know, maybe even shock. I can't understand what's been going on inside my head. I suppose it was your words, your voice, the image in my mind of you lying on the ground. The deer that almost died in the river. The horrible sounds of a saw and actual screams coming from that poor animal." Tilting her head to look into Brad's face, tears in her eyes, Juanita whispered, "And that arrow in the tree trunk, oh my God." Juanita collapsed back into Brad's arms.

With water, tissues, and the passing of a few minutes, Juanita's composure returned. The interview team ambled back into the room, uncertain as to where to focus their eyes. No one knew if anything should be said.

Juanita handled the moment with grace. Speaking with a smile, she broke the ice. "Come on in, folks. I just had a little allergy attack, that's all. Doctors tell me I'm allergic to a guy named Brad Walker. I plan to find a cure right away." She again sat in her chair, but now fully faced the rest of the room.

Juanita's humor proved to be the perfect antidote. The atmosphere felt lighter as conversation returned and seats were taken. Janice activated the recorder and initiated a return to business. "Okay, Brad, please begin where you were before the break and finish your story."

Shifting uncomfortably in his chair, Brad grinned as he began speaking. "Well, there is not a great deal more to say. I was almost finished when we decided to take that little recess."

Completing his story of how he had witnessed an owl miraculously appear and attack Birdwell, Brad waited for a response. The people in the room simply stared incredulously. Brad watched a slight smile slide onto Juanita's face. The room remained stone silent. All eyes and faces remained frozen. It was as if they had just witnessed a flock of pigs flying past the window. The young FBI agent, forgetting that the interview was being recorded, blurted the words that were in everyone's mind. "You gotta be shittin' me!"

Unable to control himself, Brad laughed openly. Raising his arms as if surrendering, he spoke while shaking his head. "I've been dreading to tell you that part, but it is exactly what happened. I promise, I'm not smart enough to make something like that up on my own."

Brad glanced to Janice. She had yet to register anything but a stunned stare. He next looked to Juanita. She smiled. They both could read the question that Janice Weathers was undoubtedly trying to process within her prosecutor's mind: *How in the world could a prosecutor ever include this in a warrant for attempted murder?*

Finally, Charles Carson managed to move things along. "Okay, Brad, what happened next?"

Grateful for the break, Brad quickly wrapped up the story of Birdwell running to his truck and speeding away. "That's it for the Birdwell part of the story. A lot more happened to rescue the wounded deer. But I'm guessing you don't need to hear that right now."

A collective sigh rippled through the room. "This has been one incredible story." Janice Weathers rose to turn off the recorder. "I have no idea how you have managed to collect yourselves after such an experience. All I can say is thank God you are here today talking with us."

Heads nodded and everyone stood. Brad stepped across the room to take Juanita's hand. "We are here in Santa Fe for the night. We plan to have dinner, enjoy a margarita or two, and then try to rest. It's been an ordeal. Tomorrow, our plans are to drive up to Taos for a day or two of relaxing. Give a call if you need anything more."

———————

Santa Fe's Plaza brimmed with energy. Tourists, enjoying the magic of early autumn in New Mexico, filled restaurants and wandered through shops. As the sun sank into the western horizon, the blush of evening glowed along Palace Avenue and San Francisco Street. Cathedral Basilica of St. Francis embraced the sun's final rays. Ancient walls of the holy structure appeared to be illuminated from within, poised to break out in glorious chorus with the heavenly host.

Juanita and Brad felt lucky to have found a room in the La Fonda Hotel on short notice. After departing the New Mexico Department of Public Safety, they had immediately driven to the hotel, checked in, and collapsed onto the bed for desperately needed sleep. Rested and recovered from the afternoon's emotionally draining proceedings, they now strolled across San Francisco Street. Entering the plaza hand in hand, they marveled at the beauty of the cathedral. Dwarfed by the plaza's monstrous trees that stood vigil over the centuries-old heart of Santa Fe, they moved slowly. Aware that they were surrounded by pure enchantment it would be a sin to rush. The oldest capital city in America deserved time.

Stopping and turning her body in a full circle, Juanita welcomed the captivation of a panoramic view. "You know what I think?" Without waiting for a reply, Juanita continued. "Santa Fe and Taos are magical for so many reasons. Artists and art lovers talk of how the light seems to simply float on the wind. When the sun touches the mountains, its light just bends. It folds over the land like a blanket." Moving her head gently, Juanita was quiet for a moment. "But there is something more than beautiful light. The body of Santa Fe and Taos, the buildings themselves, are special. To me, the buildings don't appear to have been built but rather to have grown up from the earth." She shrugged. "Maybe it's adobe, maybe it's the architecture. I don't know. But in my eyes, Santa Fe and Taos seem to be a part of the natural landscape."

"Good grief, sweetheart. You've become quite poetic." Brad laughed. "People may begin to call you the prosecuting philosopher."

"Stuff it. You know what I mean. Just look at all that surrounds us. Breathe the air. This is why we love New Mexico."

Placing an arm about Juanita's shoulders, Brad pulled her close. "I hear you. We have each other and we have New Mexico. That's good enough for me."

———

Reaching the western edge of the plaza, Lincoln Avenue was closed to traffic, allowing pedestrians to cross the street without rush or bustle. Good fortune continued. They were seated in a quiet corner of the outdoor patio of the Plaza Café. Their view of the plaza and the ethereal beauty of Cathedral Basilica of St. Francis was a perfectly orchestrated display of serenity. Without speaking or thinking, they did not take seats across the table from each other but sat side by side. The events of recent hours served as a magnet. Both of them needed for their bodies to remain in near constant contact. Juanita and Brad were keenly aware of how close they had come to this evening not happening at all—ever.

After touching glasses and savoring the first taste of tequila, salt, and lime, a brief kiss was shared. Candlelight captured a mischievous twinkle in Juanita's eyes as she gazed over the rim of her glass. "I know precisely what you are thinking, Brad Walker. You may as well go ahead and shout out to the entire plaza." Gathering salt with a seductive sweep of her tongue, Juanita again sipped her drink.

"Beautiful summer evening with a margarita. Beautiful summer evening with another margarita. You don't even care if we have dinner, do you? Your mind is back in that hotel room. And oh, my goodness, the things that are going through that mind of yours!" Juanita tossed her head back in a full, but soft, laugh. "Now, I dare you to deny anything I just said."

Leaning back in their seats, they laughed and clasped hands. Together, they looked up to the first stars now scattering across the sky. Before again speaking, Juanita gave Brad's hand a firm squeeze. "I'm all in favor of making magic in our room tonight. But this girl has got to eat first. I've not had a bite since you decided to go for a little swim in the creek yesterday. I am one hungry rancher's daughter." Placing her lips close to Brad's ear, Juanita whispered. "Buy me dinner and I am all yours."

———

When their meal was served, with a second round of margaritas, Juanita and Brad gave serious thought that they may have been granted entrance into heaven. With the spice of red chili, the earthy flavor of blue corn, and the miracle of margaritas, a sense of peace soothed their troubled spirits. For the first time in hours, Luther Birdwell's sneer, along with the images of a suffering deer and a crossbow and arrows, mercifully melted into the depths of Santa Fe's night sky.

"Before we head back to our room," Juanita said, giving Brad's hand a squeeze, "and I show you how much I love you, I need you to help me with something. Thoughts are beginning to take root and I want your opinion."

"Sounds serious."

"So much has happened in the last day or two. It is practically impossible for me to get my mind wrapped around everything."

"Good grief. Tell me something I don't already know."

"What happened to me with a visitor from another world is enough in itself to blow a person's mind. Then, you find yourself staring straight into the eyes of the Grim Reaper." Juanita stopped speaking. Eyes glistening with emotion, she finished her thought. "Before being saved by an owl. . ." Juanita moved her head side to side. "Something is going on here. I can't explain it. I'm frustrated but I'm also frightened."

"I hear you, baby. I hear you." Extending a hand, Brad softly brushed her cheek with a finger.

"But with every passing hour, I am more convinced that things are happening that are beyond us." Juanita lifted her face to the sky, lowered her voice to a whisper, and spoke to the stars. "I've already said this, Brad. But I'm telling you again. Someone or something is talking to us. We need to be listening or paying attention. I don't know what's happening, but we can't just pretend everything is normal. The past couple of days have been anything but normal."

Inhaling a powerful breath, Brad moved his chair and shifted his weight to bring his body closer to Juanita. "How in the world could I disagree? You are absolutely right about the mystery of what we have experienced. But you say you have thoughts that are taking root. In the name of heaven, my brain is so muddled, nothing could possibly take root. I don't know where or how to begin to make sense of a damned thing."

"I don't know how to unravel things either. But I have replayed that woman's words a million times." Juanita paused. "It wasn't just some woman, Brad. It was me. It was me talking to me. It was like standing in front of a mirror and having a conversation with the reflection."

Candlelight from their table captured the uncertainty swirling within Juanita's eyes. Brad reached for her hand.

"I can hear her voice right now. I hear the words she spoke. But those words are my words, spoken by me to me." Juanita's voice assumed a slow and deliberate cadence as she recited to Brad from memory. "'You and I are very lucky to be given these chances. Be thankful that you are able to finish the life that was taken from you. Make each day count.'"

Juanita closed her eyes, sealing the moment. "That is exactly what she said. I'm trying to understand her meaning. Am I missing something? If so, then what in the world is it? What am I missing? What am I supposed to do?"

Neither of them spoke. Answers felt out of reach, and there was nothing to say. A faint smile returning to her face, Juanita broke the somber mood with a friendly poke to Brad's chest. "But you tell me something. How in the world am I supposed to decipher all this stuff while you are absolutely determined to get yourself killed?"

Giving a hint of a shrug and moving his head, Brad simply looked at Juanita without replying.

"Really, Brad, this is a heck of lot coming all at once. When I close my eyes and try to sort things out, I have no idea what image is going to appear. Will it be my visitor from another place and time?" Her voice softened. "Or will I see the arrow that came so close to taking you away from me?"

Silence. Candlelight. Starlight.

"I wish I knew what to say, Juanita." Brad's voice was scarcely above a whisper. "We both need help with this. I am just as lost as you." Brad shifted in his body. "I'm trying to think logically but, honestly, logical thought may not be any good here." Inhaling and releasing a thoughtful sigh, Brad continued. "Your Uncle Foster has closed his shop for a few days. He is heading here to Santa Fe to talk with someone about the pottery that started this whole mess. The shop is locked up tight and I'm comfortable with what we have planned. Let's spend a day or two in Taos. We need a day for relaxing and thinking. Something tells me that is the best idea for now."

Leaning forward, Juanita brought her face to within an inch of Brad's. "Time in Taos to unwind does sound like a marvelous idea." Juanita smiled. "But it does not hold a candle to how much I want to just spend some time with you."

———

Lifting coffee mugs in a morning toast, Juanita and Brad welcomed the energy of natural light pouring in from abundant skylights. Sounds of cascading water drifted from the water feature of Hotel La Fonda's La Plazuela Café. Bustle of morning's rush within the hotel's lobby was a pleasantly muted welcome to the new day. For decades, people of fame from all walks of life had gathered under the roof of La Fonda's hotel and café. When dining here, Brad always allowed himself the fantasy that he occupied the very table where Robert Oppenheimer, along with other scientists of the Manhattan Project, had strategized America's hope to end the Second World War with the atomic bomb.

In the minds of Juanita and Brad, a more perfect setting for sharing sopapillas and honey could not be imagined. The serenity they were content to enjoy without conversation was interrupted by the simultaneous vibrating of their cell phones. Silence ensued as they each read the text message that had appeared on their screens.

**Laboratory and fingerprint exams complete.**

**Positive full and partial print matches from arrow and beer cans recovered at park ranger's murder scene and from arrows and crossbow used during assault on Brad.**

**Luther Birdwell's prints on all.**

**Arrow used to wound the deer and arrow recovered from tree trunk are identical to arrow manufacture from murder scene.**

**Warrant charging Birdwell for murder of Federal Officer on Federal Reservation will be issued by U.S. Magistrate this morning.**
**Will leave decision concerning attempted murder of Brad to discretion of local prosecutors.**

**You guys be cautious.**

**No idea of Birdwell's whereabouts but once**

**the manhunt begins, he will quickly learn of his fugitive status.**

**The man is crazy.**

**Take your time to decompress and, Juanita, we miss you here in the office.**

**Janice**

The relaxed mood of their morning slipped away with the reading of the text message. Juanita and Brad each contemplated the ramifications of the message. What they had anticipated had now become reality. The man who had tried to murder Brad was now the subject of a manhunt. What this meant for the future was unknown.

Juanita was the first to speak. "I think I need to call Uncle Foster and let him know. I don't know when he plans to reopen the shop, but this may factor into his decision."

Giving a nod of agreement, Brad gathered his thoughts. "I think you are right. Tell your uncle to keep things locked up and stay away from the shop until things settle. You and I need to figure our own plans for when to return."

"We have the living quarters of the shop for as long as we wish so we can return any time. That pottery is still locked up in his safe. I have no idea what to think about Birdwell trying to get it back. It is obviously something of value, but what the man is willing to risk is an unknown." Juanita was thoughtful for a moment. "I'm fine to spend a few more days there and help keep an eye on things." Juanita sipped her coffee. "Also, I am not super excited about returning to my office just yet. I need a few more days away from Albuquerque and courtroom stuff. I want a little more time to think about all that has happened to us."

"Letting your uncle know the latest is a good idea. We will take all the time you need before returning to Albuquerque. Having you jump back into the rat race is not a priority." Brad reached across the table to touch Juanita's hand. "Take all the time you need."

Juanita's eyes and face spoke her gratitude.

"I can't predict what Birdwell's next move will be, but your friend, Janice, is absolutely right when she says Birdwell is crazy." Brad swirled coffee in his mug before continuing. "I agree that the man is crazy, but I doubt that he is stupid. It will take very little time before his relatives and every known hangout or associate from his past will be receiving a visit by someone from law enforcement. The bushes are going to start shaking. It's only a matter of hours until he will know that he is a wanted man."

"I agree," Juanita replied over her coffee mug. "That's what gives me some comfort about him not wanting to show up at the gift shop. Being a fugitive from a murder charge will send him scurrying."

"Birdwell for sure knows that his presence around Red River is no secret. The red pickup truck that almost ran over Uncle Ernie's neighbor after killing that deer has also got to be a part of the story." Brad leaned over the table, bringing his face closer to Juanita. "I may be dead-ass wrong, but I think it would be pure stupidity for Birdwell, and whoever he is running with, to stay in the area. By the time the sun sets tonight, Birdwell, and whoever he is running with, will know that the heat is on. My money says they will be in the wind before dawn tomorrow. Where they will go, I haven't a clue."

"I think you are right. But I can't help but worry for my uncle. He is holding something that is valuable to Birdwell. Who knows what a person who is evil and desperate, not to mention crazy, might do."

"I can't argue, and I understand how you feel." Brad leaned back in his chair. "If your uncle can afford to keep the shop closed and stay the heck away for a few days, I think that is the best plan for the short term. If Birdwell happens to get locked up right away, that solves the problem." Brad shook his head. "Beyond that, I'm not sure what's best."

With a shrug of her shoulders, Juanita replied, "Uncle Foster does not run his shop for money. He does it because he loves his merchandise, and he loves talking with all the people who come in. He can easily stay closed for a few days until things settle. His wife is still off visiting relatives in in Texas, so he is alone right now. He will handle his business in Santa Fe to find someone to place a value on the pottery before heading home. I suspect he will probably go out to torment his brother, Uncle Ernie, and be a rancher again for a few days."

"Okay, good plan. Make the phone call to Uncle Foster to give him the latest. Let's finish up here, pack our bags, and head up to Taos. I feel strongly about you and me spending some time together." Brad cocked his head to one side. "You know, sweetheart, you are not the only one trying to figure things out. I have a few demons of my own that I'm struggling with. I love Taos. I think the key to my peace of mind may very well be there. Somewhere beneath Taos Mountain, this old cowboy is going to find some answers. I want to talk with you about some stuff that I've been putting off. Please, stay with me on this. Give me a little more time and I will explain. Stick with me, please."

Juanita's eyes twinkled in a manner that Brad had not seen since the afternoon of her strange visitor. "I plan to stay with you until the world stops turning, you old cowboy. I hate to deliver the bad news, but I am saddled up and ready to ride. You are stuck with me until you ride off into the sunset."

The familiar quiver rippled through Brad's heart.

———

Retracing their trip of the previous day, Juanita and Brad once again drove with only sporadic conversation. Upon reaching Taos, the historic district of narrow streets and adobe walls delivered the charm and charisma they so loved. Driving beneath the canopy of cottonwood, elm, and weeping willow trees that shaded Upper Ranchitos Road, they lowered the windows of Brad's truck to breathe the purity of the morning. A sharp bend to the right transformed the wooded terrain into one of open meadows. Chamisa stood in gigantic clusters. Yellow blossoms brimmed in brilliance beneath the cobalt blue of a Taos sky. Swells of clouds floated, casting ever-changing shadows over the sacred canyons of Taos Mountain.

"This is absolutely gorgeous." Brad pulled to the side of the road. "Oh, my Lord, Juanita, we have to get out of this stuffy truck and feel what is around us."

Aware of the history and the beauty of all that surrounded her, Juanita exited the truck. Holding her cell phone, she rotated her body in increments, attempting to capture in photographs the enchantment of the moment. "Photos never do justice to times like this, but they provide Technicolor memories for me." She smiled. "And since I am the only one here who matters, that is reason enough for a thousand photos."

"Absolutely. Take your time. Soak everything in. Stash it away for a rainy day."

Once inside the vehicle, Juanita and Brad sat without speaking. Windows still down, a breeze moved over their faces. "I can't decide where to look." Juanita laughed her beautiful laugh. "If I spend time admiring the Chamisa, I miss the changing hues on Taos Mountain. Oh, my God, Brad, I am so happy that we came here. This is so beautiful."

More moments of introspection followed. Neither wanted to break the bewitching spell of the magic they were experiencing. Finally, Juanita again spoke. Her gaze remained fixed on the outside, toward Taos Mountain, but she directed her words to Brad. "Why is it that every time I come here, my soul feels at peace? Why is it that when I am in Taos, things feel so familiar? The streets, the houses, even trees and the land are like old friends." Juanita turned to face Brad. "When I am here, whether alone or with you, I feel a sense that I have come home." Juanita closed her eyes as she reached for Brad's hand. "I don't know how to explain my feelings. But when I am in Taos, a voice speaks to me. A voice that tells me a part of my heart is close to that beautiful mountain we are looking at." Juanita returned her gaze to the Chamisa and Taos Mountain. "I don't know, Brad. I just can't explain it."

Brad did not offer a quick response. He was uncertain about

what to say and he sensed that Juanita needed a few moments with her own thoughts. When he felt that enough time had elapsed, Brad eased into a reply. "I wish I could see into the past or peer into the future. But, since I can't do that, all I know to say is that you have had way too much thrown at you in recent days. I can't explain your feelings. But I've learned the hard way, never blow it off when you think a hidden voice is speaking. Those little voices have spoken to me in the past. Thank God I listened. It was hidden voices that brought you and me together. I love you, Juanita. I will hold your hand no matter what those voices say or where they lead you."

Extending her body across the truck's cab, Juanita placed her lips onto Brad's. Nothing more needed to be said. It was time to go.

————

Continuing on Upper Ranchitos Road, they reached their destination, a single-story structure of Southwestern hacienda architecture sitting on over an acre of sage and Chamisa-covered land. Sculptures placed about the landscape welcomed visitors to the Millicent Rogers Museum. Both Juanita and Brad had visited the museum previously, but it had been several years. Earlier, while driving from Santa Fe, they had talked about Millicent Rogers. A young woman and heiress to a vast fortune, she ultimately left her New York home to settle in Taos. Millicent Rogers became legendary as a collector of Southwest treasures and a preserving force of Native American and Southwest history and culture. Juanita and Brad agreed that the quiet atmosphere of her museum was just what the doctor ordered as an antidote to the frenzied experiences of the past days. The wisdom of their decision quickly became manifest. Meandering from room to room, they were gifted with glimpses into the history of Taos and all of the Southwest. Softly illuminated displays set a tone of respect and quiet intimacy. It was exactly what they had hoped for.

A display of turquoise jewelry temporarily mesmerized Brad. He had always felt that turquoise represented the soul of Mother Earth. Nuggets of blue and green, streaked in hues of copper, transcended life itself in Brad's mind. Feeling Juanita's grasp on his arm, he interrupted his focus on the turquoise. "Come with me." Juanita's voice was an excited whisper. "The most amazing letter I have ever read is right over here." Holding Brad's arm, Juanita guided him to an adjoining room where she stopped and pointed to an enlarged version of a printed document. "Read this. The words are exactly what we talked about a bit ago. They are about Taos, its beauty, and a sense of belonging. I swear, what is written here echo my sentiments perfectly. I only wish I were poetic enough to express myself so beautifully."

Stepping closer, Brad saw that the display was a letter that had been written by Millicent Rogers to her son, shortly before her death. Her son, Paul, had given the museum permission to reprint the letter.

Reading glasses in place and Juanita's grip firmly about his arm, Brad moved close to the document.

*Darling Paulie,*

*Did I ever tell you about the feeling I had a little while ago? Suddenly passing Taos Mountain I felt that I was part of the earth, so that I felt the sun on my surface and the rain. I felt the stars and the growth of the moon, under me, rivers ran. And against me were the tides. The waters of rain sank into me. And I thought if I stretched out my hands they would be earth and green would grow from me. And I knew that there was no reason to be lonely that one was everything, and Death was as easy as the rising sun and as calm and natural – that to be enfolded in Earth was not an end but part of oneself, part of every day and night that we lived, so that Being part of the earth one was never alone. And all the fear went out of me – with a great good stillness and strength.*

*If anything should happen to me, now, ever, just remember all this. I want to be buried in Taos with the wide sky – .... One has so little time to be still, to lie still and look at the Earth and the changing colours and the forest – and the voices of people and clouds and light on water, smells and sound of music and the taste of wood smoke in the air.*

*.... I've had a most lovely life to myself – I've enjoyed it as thoroughly as it could be enjoyed. And when my time comes, no one is to feel that I have lost anything of it – or be too sorry – I've been in all of you – and will go on Being. So remember it peacefully – take all the good things that your life put there in your eyes – and they, your family, children, will see through your eyes. My love to all of you.*

"Wow! That's one powerful letter." Brad turned to Juanita who was watching him closely. "Beautiful writing for sure but this is deeper than simply crafting poetic sentences. There is lots to think about in those words."

Smiling, Juanita nodded in agreement. "After my visitor from the other side and your brush with actually crossing over to the other side, that letter could have been written to you or me."

Together, Juanita and Brad gave the letter another silent read. The depth of thought in the expressions of a woman who recognized that her days were limited struck them as especially poignant. In silent contemplation, Juanita and Brad moved on to the next room. Pottery by Maria Martinez, the famed potter of New Mexico's San Ildefonso Pueblo, created an aura of sanctuary. Marveling in the excellence of her work, they took time, relishing the experience and their time together. But as they admired the works of a master, uninvited worries found a crack. A reminder of things not so beautiful wormed into their minds. Thoughts of the pottery currently secured in Uncle Foster's safe took root. Heaven only knew its history or value. The serenity of the morning faded into a foggy mist of disquiet. Images of Luther Birdwell took shape within the mist. The beauty created by the hands of Maria Martinez faded.

———

Once again in the heart of the historic district of Taos, Juanita and Brad sat beneath the shade of an umbrella. From the patio of their café, traffic of Paseo Pueblo Del Norte hummed. Iced tea and salads were delivered to their table as Juanita cast a questioning look to Brad. "So, what is it that you hope to find in the Kit Carson Cemetery?" Juanita's question was the only logical response after being told by Brad that he wanted to walk across the street and explore the site of Kit Carson's grave.

An uncomfortable shift in his chair and a sudden fascination with his shoes was all the body language Juanita needed to see. Brad was holding back. She remained quiet but her gaze became focused. "Talk to me, Brad Walker. You said earlier that you had something on your mind. You asked for more time. I'm thinking you've had your time. What is it that you need to say to me? What are you looking for?"

With a sigh, Brad met Juanita's eyes and spoke. "Yes, I am looking for something." Hesitation tinged his voice. "I'm trying to be logical and think straight about things of the past days. Just like you, I have thought a million times about your visitor at the shop. I can't begin to explain things, but I believe everything that you saw and heard that day was absolutely real."

With a slight nod, Juanita's scrutiny continued.

"You brought it up last night at dinner. We cannot possibly ignore the things that have happened to us simply because we can't explain or understand those things."

Another nod from Juanita.

"What finally caused something to click inside my head is how the woman reminded you that it was Manuel's sister who cared for me. I think the woman who spoke to you gave several clues about the purpose of her visit. But it was that one line about Manuel that really jolted me. And also what she said about the famous scout. Those were words with meaning. Hidden meaning, perhaps, but she delivered a message when she said those things."

Her eyes boring into Brad, Juanita spoke. "I think I understand. You are thinking she was referring to the scout, Kit Carson? He is buried here in Taos. In fact, his grave is right across the street." Juanita's eyes widened. "Oh, my God!"

Again, Brad shifted his body and failed to meet Juanita's eyes. Clearly uncomfortable, he breathed deeply, summoning courage. "I've had this on my mind for a couple of days. But there was never the right time to talk with you. I think we are going to find something in that cemetery. If we find what I think we are going to find, it won't answer everything. In fact, it may create even more questions. But I have to go. I have no choice but to go and look. I want you with me. If we find what I think we will find, I'm going to tell you about some things that happened to me before we were together. Some things just as profound as your visitor."

"What in the world are you talking about?" Juanita stared at Brad, puzzled urgency radiating from her face.

"As much as I love you, Juanita, there is a part of my past that you don't know. I have never known how to tell you or had the courage to even try."

Following a scrutinizing stare at Brad, Juanita uttered a response. "Of course, I'll go with you. But I don't understand. Why now? If something is so confounding, why have you never mentioned it? What's going on, Brad?"

"Maybe it's because I'm carrying a bit of shame. All that's in my mind may turn out to be more of a confession than a revelation." Moving his head from side to side, Brad's shoulders slumped. "Because I could not explain something, I buried my head in the sand and ignored it. I know now, that has been a mistake. I will no longer allow myself to continue on that road. The words that woman spoke to you in Uncle Foster's shop are so close to words that were spoken to me. . ." Brad's voice faded as he looked at Juanita. "I would be lying if I told you I don't have some fear of what we may be about to learn. But I can't ignore the mystery any longer." Nodding his head toward Paseo Pueblo Del Norte, Brad spoke. "I need to cross that street. I need you to be with me."

Straightening her body, Juanita lifted her glass, taking a long swallow of iced tea.

Silence felt eternal to Brad as he gave time for her to consider what had just been said.

Setting the glass back on the table, Juanita spoke with authority. "Well, Brad Walker, what are we waiting for? Let's cross that street."

———

After crossing the street from their café, Juanita and Brad entered Kit Carson Memorial Park. Very few people were in the park midday and midweek. Moving beneath gigantic trees, they headed toward the cemetery that was a part of the park. As they approached and gravestones came into view, Juanita reached for Brad's arm and stopped. Standing still and looking at the panorama of land and sky, she took a few seconds to absorb all that surrounded them. "Can you imagine how this must have looked when the first bodies were buried here?" Juanita pointed to Taos Mountain. "Nothing but a few buildings of mud and that big old giant standing guard, day and night. In some ways it seems terribly lonely. But in other ways absolutely beautiful. This makes me think about that letter we just read in the museum. Millicent Rogers wrote to her son telling him that Taos was definitely where she wished to be buried. She obviously saw this place as beautiful, not lonely."

"You are absolutely right." Brad grasped Juanita's hand as they again walked.

A simple fence of black wrought iron defined the boundary of the cemetery. Upon entering, Juanita and Brad were surprised at the small size of the area that defined the burial ground. "I expected something much larger." Juanita drifted her eyes over the field of gravestones and monuments. "This is only a couple of acres or so."

"I didn't know what to expect," Brad said as his eyes swept over the area. "But now that we are here, I'm happy to see we can explore the entire cemetery in a reasonable amount of time. It should be fairly easy."

Following a well-defined pathway, Juanita and Brad meandered. Some graves were manicured, others lay in diminished memory of lives and times long departed. Bouquets of plastic flowers sprinkled the grounds in splotches of faded color. Many of the graves were marked unpretentiously. Others bore elaborate monuments, documenting military or religious influence in the early days of New Mexico. Beneath a cluster of headstones, the graves of Kit Carson, his wife, and children dominated the western perimeter of the cemetery.

After describing to Juanita what he was looking for or what he hoped to find, Brad took a deep breath. "I don't know for certain, but I'm pretty sure it will be a modest stone marker." Brad moved his eyes over the cemetery in a methodical evaluation. Pointing to a far corner, he continued. "Let's start over there and work our way from end to end. Then, we will reverse and come back again in the opposite direction. We just have to look at every grave."

Progress was relatively fast as the grounds were flat and free of overgrowing brush or trees. After two trips from border to border without finding a grave that matched what they sought, Juanita suddenly stopped. Lifting a hand over her eyes to diminish glare, she bent her body over a grave. "Brad, come over here. Take a look at this."

Together, they examined a crude marker that certainly was not a formal gravestone. It looked to be a stone that had been gathered from the surrounding terrain and then modified into a memorial. The marker had been placed flat onto the ground with no means of support. Passing years had taken a toll. The stone had settled into the ground. Dirt and clumps of grass practically concealed the entire memorial.

"Good eyes, Juanita. I'm not sure I would have spotted this."

Dropping to her knees, Juanita lowered her face close as she examined her discovery. Using bare fingers, she brushed soil and years of blackened grime from the stone's surface. Brad, also now on his knees, focused light from his cell phone to illuminate what Juanita was exposing. Bending their backs until their faces were only inches from the marker, they unconsciously held their breath. Juanita's hands swept away final remnants of dirt and debris while Brad directed light. Letter by letter, etched word by etched word, a message that had been entombed for over a century rose to the eyes of Juanita and Brad.

*Manuel Lujan and his beloved sister, Juanita*
*Together they died*
*so that children*
*could live*
*January 1847*

Their bodies hovering, Juanita and Brad stared at their discovery. Collective breathing and pounding hearts hung in suspended silence. Cool dampness from the disturbed soil touched their faces.

"Oh, my God, Juanita, this is it." Brad straightened his back. Juanita followed. Their eyes met. Conversation of a thousand words was exchanged without a sound being uttered.

Gripping hands, Juanita and Brad stood together. Without speaking and hands intertwined, they walked to a nearby bench where they practically collapsed as they sat. Juanita did not speak. But when she looked to Brad, her eyes were somewhere between pleading for answers and fear of what those answers might hold.

Following a huge inhale, Brad broke the silence. "Okay, it's confession time." With hesitation, and looking up into the sky, he began to speak. "As I have told you, I've never been comfortable in sharing this with another person. But after what happened in your uncle's shop, the time for secrets is over."

"I have no idea what you are about to say to me, but my visitor made it clear that you and I are both a part of her message." Juanita paused. "Message or mystery, whatever, I want to know. Please talk to me."

"Think back to when you and I were being drawn to each other. Neither of us could understand our feelings. I guess we were falling in love without any idea of how or why. I drove to your parents' ranch and met them for the first time. Your mom laid out a feast as only a rancher's wife can do. Then we drove all around the ranch and spent magical time, just talking. Remember that windmill and the beautiful sunset we watched?"

"Oh, yes, I remember. I think we were already in love that evening. We were both just so overwhelmed with the crazy feelings that we had known each other sometime before. We didn't know what to think."

"You lost your mother's pendant in my truck that evening. Having that turquoise stone, and knowing it came from you. . . " Brad moved his head. "You have no idea how much I felt your spirit in that pendant."

Juanita replied with a smile and a nod.

"During our time together that day, you asked me to look into the suicide of a friend you had known in law school. I did as you asked, and man-oh-man, did that ever lead to an adventure. Your friend had become involved with a young girl being manipulated for sexual exploitation. The tragedy of that poor girl, Lucy Hernandez, will be with me forever. She took her own life. It must have been more than your friend could bear because shortly after Lucy's death, he ended his life also. Before I knew it, I was up to my ears in a case of child exploitation that was absolutely heart-breaking."

"Oh, yes. Those days seem like yesterday."

Drawing and exhaling a hard breath, Brad continued. "Here is the part that I've never told you, or anyone else. The reason that I was able to finally resolve that whole mess is due to an experience very much like what you had with the visitor in the gift shop."

Juanita looked to Brad. Her eyes and face transformed into a single question mark.

"The key to the entire mystery came from an old man in an Albuquerque nursing home. His name," Brad made a slight nodding gesture toward the gravestone, "was Manuel Lujan."

Juanita said nothing but her eyes became even more intense.

"Manuel Lujan had been like a grandfather to Lucy Hernandez. That is why I went to the nursing home. I was seeking his help to understand things about Lucy's life that could have contributed to her suicide." Placing fingers over the bridge of his nose and closing his eyes, Brad lowered his head. "When I met Manuel Lujan, it became an out-of-this-world experience, Juanita. Nothing like it had ever happened to me before." He paused. "And nothing like it since. That is until your visitor in the shop a few days ago."

Juanita simply gaped at Brad.

"Manuel Lujan was close to death." Brad's voice changed tone. "I am absolutely convinced that somebody out there," Brad lifted his head and looked to the sky, "somebody out there had a hand in taking me to him before he passed. I don't know, Juanita, maybe that somebody out there told him not to die until I came." Brad closed his eyes as his shoulders shrugged. "I don't know which it was, but one of the two damned sure happened."

"I'm listening, sweetheart. I'm listening and I'm feeling your distress."

"Manuel Lujan actually told me that he had been expecting my visit. He said that he had been waiting for me. I was absolutely dumbfounded. When I asked about Lucy Hernandez, he told me about a diary that Lucy kept. He said that the diary would contain clues to help unravel her tragedy."

Not even a blink came from Juanita's eyes.

"Then he began talking about things that he saw in my future. He said that I would be tested and face an evil serpent. He told me this was going to happen beneath the ground and in darkness." Brad lifted his arms and shoulders in bewilderment. "He told me that I was the only person who could do what had to be done. Then, if things couldn't get any crazier, Manuel Lujan pulled a handwritten letter out of a drawer beside his bed. This was something that he had prepared sometime earlier. He didn't know me or anything about me, but he said that he had been saving it for me. I'll never forget how he looked or how I felt when his quivering old hand handed me that letter. I had no idea what was happening."

Brad stopped speaking as he paused and looked into Juanita's face. "But I can damned sure tell you that when that letter touched my fingers, there was somebody in that room besides me and an old man."

"Oh, my God, Brad."

"I have the letter that he gave me. It is hidden in a safe place. I promise you, that is one thing that I will never let slip away."

Juanita reached to touch Brad's hand.

"But I also took a photograph, just in case. I have it right here." Scrolling through his phone, Brad's thumb ceased moving when he found what he needed. "Here it is. I made this photo as soon as I left the nursing home that day. Read it, Juanita. You are about to be blown right out of this world."

A tentative expression shaping her face, Juanita accepted Brad's cellphone. Settling back into the bench, she turned her eyes to the screen. Penciled writing, obviously from a shaky hand, looked back. Juanita tracked the downward slanted lines that had been scrawled across a lined paper.

*I have asked but answers were not given*
*Only you can do this*
*The people of the Parajito await you*
*They will speak but you must go to them*
*They are angry*
*Listen for their voices*
*Only at night can they be heard*
*You have tasted their water before*
*It always flows*
*Drink it again*
*You will be alone when you face the serpent*
*He lives near the fire*

Juanita seemed unable to tear her eyes away from the screen. She read and reread, never glancing up or acknowledging the presence of Brad. Brad gave her time. He sat quietly, his focus on Taos Mountain.

When she finally returned Brad's phone, Juanita waited seconds before she spoke. "What in the world did this mean? What did you think when you read this? What in the name of heaven does it mean now?" Her face seeking answers, Juanita waited. At this point, it was all on Brad.

Brad lifted his phone and looked at the image on the screen. How many times had he scrutinized the words? Too many to count.

Slipping the cell phone into his shirt pocket, it was Brad's turn to take time before replying. He shrugged. "At the time, I had no idea what any of the letter meant. It took some thinking and a bit of imagination, but gradually I pieced it together. The Parajito Plateau is a huge area down by Los Alamos that encompasses the ruins of Bandelier. A civilization thrived there, hundreds of years ago. Their homes were carved out of cliff facings or constructed from stone and mud. People who study that stuff think that the main reason the area was settled was because of the creek that runs through the valley. Frijoles Creek. It never goes dry. Having a reliable water supply was a big deal."

Juanita took an opportunity to interject. "I know Bandelier. I love it there."

"Yeah, me too." Brad seemed to speak to the sagebrush, Chamisa, and Taos Mountain as he looked straight ahead. "I took the words of Manuel Lujan literally. Since I had been to Bandelier before, I took his letter to mean that I should go back and do so at night. I hiked into Bandelier in late afternoon. All the tourists were leaving, so I soon found myself to be the only person in the midst of those ancient ruins. As the sun sank, the canyon practically glowed in the last minutes of fading light. Everything seemed surreal. You have no idea how alone and out of place I felt. I was an intruder. I swear, Juanita, I could feel eyes from within those caves and crumbling ruins. Some sort of beings or spirits were peering out at me. I still get the shivers every time I think about it."

"I'm feeling the shivers just hearing you tell the story."

"After a while, I found a comfortable place to settle until I figured things out. I was beneath a cottonwood tree, right beside the creek. Once twilight faded and night really set in, the sky turned black beyond words. The stars were brilliant, more than anything you can imagine. It was a heck of an experience. Half of my life has been spent outdoors so night skies are nothing new to me. But that night was unlike anything I had ever seen or felt before. Bandelier is alive, I don't care what anyone says, the place holds life. Being within those ruins, alone at night, was a feeling I will never forget. In some ways it was magical. But in other ways, it was scary as hell and absolutely haunting."

"I know exactly what that canyon and those ruins look like. I'm still shivering."

"Yeah, it was something. I had Manuel Lujan's letter with me. I read it again and again, trying to get straight in my head what the heck I was doing. Finally, I just did what the letter told me to do. I drank from the creek." Brad leaned forward, placing his forearms on his legs. "I don't know what to think about what happened next. After drinking from the creek, I simply fell asleep. Maybe I had a dream." Brad moved his head from side to side. "But I'll never really believe that. It was way too real. In my dream, or whatever it was, I was in the depths of Bandelier Canyon, but the ruins were alive with people. Fires were burning inside caves. I could hear voices and see shadows of people moving about. The smell of smoke from campfires was all around me. I don't know how long I was in the dream." Brad looked to Juanita. "If it was a dream."

"Good God, Brad."

"But when I awakened, or returned to the real world, two things were very different. Instead of a black sky filled with stars, a full moon had risen. The cliffs were illuminated almost like day." Brad looked to Juanita. "The second thing different was that my clothes were completely saturated with campfire smoke."

"Oh, my God." Juanita's words were whispered.

"You ain't heard the end of this yet." Brad gave Juanita a weak smile. "When I looked up at the face of the cliff, shadows cast from the moonlight were absolutely vibrant. Fissures and cracks ran all across the cliff. It looked like a fractured mirror. But then, all of a sudden, a pattern became clear to me. It was bizarre. The cracks in the cliff formed a perfect replica of a road map that I had recently seen in a police officer's quarters. It was a map of an area up in the corner of New Mexico. Not far from your parents' ranch, actually."

Brad again looked hard at Juanita. She returned his intensity.

"And what in the world do you think is a major feature of that area?"

"I know exactly what it is." Juanita moved her head in disbelief. "It's the fire mentioned in Manuel Lujan's letter. The Mount Capulin volcano." She smiled a knowing smile.

"Wiseass."

Juanita leaned into Brad with a hug.

"So, from Bandelier, I went charging up to this Mount Capulin. One heck of a storm hit while I was there. But from the top of Capulin, I was able spot a ranch house that perfectly fit the description of a ranch house that had been described by Lucy Hernandez in her diary. It was the location of her abuse."

"Unbelievable." Juanita no longer whispered but spoke out loud in amazement.

"Yep. If I had not lived this myself, I would sure as hell say unbelievable. In spite of the storm, I made it to the ranch house." Brad made a huge inhale. "And that is where the rest of Manuel Lujan's words turned out to be uncanny." Clearly uncomfortable, Brad shifted his body and spoke softly. "All I can say is that Manuel Lujan's prophecy about being tested and facing an evil serpent sure as hell came true. I was beneath the ground and in darkness. That was one awful day."

Juanita and Brad allowed some time to pass without talking. They watched in silence as afternoon clouds drifting over Taos Mountain cast ever-changing shadows. Parts of the mountain appeared to be submerged in ocean depths, others basked in fluorescence of the sun.

Brad leaned back, took a breath, and continued. "Not too long after all of this happened, I went back to visit the parents of Lucy Hernandez. It turned out that after Manuel Lujan passed away in the nursing home, he had been buried on their property. We went together to visit his grave. After that, I met you for our horse trip into the mountains. That's when you had your first introduction to a bunch of my friends." His voice lowered to a whisper. "And we've been together ever since."

Leaning her body into Brad for an embrace, they held each other as memories flowed.

Rising from the bench, Juanita faced Brad with a mischievous smile. "I suppose that just this once, I will forgive you for keeping a secret from me." With a pointing finger, she continued. "But never again. Never again. Got it?"

Arms of surrender in the air, Brad conceded. "Never again. You have my word."

"Fine. Now that we have that little issue settled, let's think about this." Juanita began pacing. Remaining seated, Brad watched her restless, back-and-forth march. When she halted, Juanita stood directly in front of Brad. "I think I'm glad that we discovered the headstone. I know I'm glad that you shared your story with me." Shaking her head in frustration, she again paced. A few steps away from the bench, Juanita turned sharply, leveled her gaze directly at Brad and spoke. "But all I see are more questions." Pointing to the recently discovered grave marker, Juanita's next words were uttered in frustration. "What the heck does that mean? Who are the children? How and why did two people named Manuel and Juanita die to save them?"

Standing to face Juanita, Brad considered his reply. "I can't answer your questions. But. . ."

Interrupting Brad, Juanita's voice rose. "And how in the world is anyone supposed to make sense of something wild and crazy as what you just told me about some old man in a nursing home? Dammit, Brad. I'm not stupid. I'm a lawyer. I have years of experience. I am a logical person. I understand facts. I understand evidence. But all of this," Juanita waved her arms in a circling motion over the cemetery, "hocus-pocus, beyond-the-grave, predicting-the-future stuff is more than I can comprehend." Juanita's eyes flashed. Any person that you or I know, any logical person, with a gram of common sense, would say we've been chewing mushrooms for even imagining this."

"You are absolutely right. That is why I've never told another person about the old man, his predictions, or his letter."

There did not seem to be anything more to say. Juanita paced, struggling to get her mind around Brad's revelations. Walking back to the grave, Brad dropped to a knee as he again read the inscribed words. He looked up to Taos Mountain. He thought of the letter written by Millicent Rogers. For how many centuries had the giant watched over life and death? How many souls were now a part of the mountain and this vast land, this vast sky?

Returning to Juanita, Brad reached for her hand as he spoke. "I do have an idea. Something that has been rolling around inside my head ever since the afternoon of your mysterious visitor." Pausing, Brad gathered his thoughts. "Remember that piece of art in our bedroom. The one we comment on almost daily?"

"Of course. The one with the old couple walking together through autumn leaves."

"Yes, that's it. The artist is Ed Romero. He called that particular piece *Autumn Leaves of Home.* I bought it for us because I thought it represented you and I going through life together."

"You were so right. I love it."

"Well, like I told you the day I brought it home, Ed and I became friends long before you and I were together. I have promised several times to introduce you to Ed, but we've never taken the time to make that happen."

"His work is amazing and yes, I would love to meet him. But how does this connect with what has happened here in this graveyard?"

"Ed is amazing in so many ways. He is much more than a man who creates beautiful images on canvas. He views the world and all of life as a canvas. In his mind, every person is an artist who paints the canvas of their life. He believes that people choose the brush and the colors that define who they are. Ed has a heart, soul, and wisdom that go beyond anyone I have ever known."

"I'm listening." Juanita waited.

"Ed's ancestors lived in this land long before this modern world of today. Their bones are a part of the very soil Taos stands on. Their blood still runs through his veins, and Ed just knows things. I don't know how he does it, but he has a way of seeing aspects of life that most people are blind to. I want to talk with him, Juanita. I think he can help us."

Juanita listened. Her thoughts formulating, she did not rush a response. Sounds of life from nearby streets seemed miles distant. A breeze stirred through the elm and cottonwoods, settling over silent graves. Brad and the cemetery remained silent. Taos Mountain watched, waiting for Juanita's reply.

Her eyes shimmering in afternoon sun, Juanita looked into Brad's face. Applying pressure to his hand, she answered. "Yes, by all means. Please, Brad, let's talk with this man. We need to talk with him as soon as we can."

# EIGHT

"THIS IS BREATHTAKING!" The morning breeze rippled blossoms of the Chamisa-filled meadow. Standing in the entrance to Ed Romero's art studio, Juanita held the mug of tea that Romero had offered. The magic of autumn in New Mexico was clearly working its spell on Juanita. She closed her eyes, hoping to forever trap the image within her mind.

"Brad has been my friend for years. To meet the woman who brings him such happiness is an honor. Thank you for visiting with me this morning." Ed Romero spoke softly as he stood beside Juanita.

Turning to face the famous artist, Juanita looked into eyes that were almost black. A mustache, trimmed with such precision that it appeared to have been drawn with a pencil, arched over a smile that seemed to never leave his face. But mostly, it was Ed's eyes that fascinated Juanita. When he looked at her, she felt his vision going straight to her soul. Juanita had a disquieting feeling that it would be impossible to keep a secret from this man.

"Oh my, Ed. Thank you for giving us your time. We both treasure your art. I just never dreamed that I would have an opportunity to meet the man himself."

Ed's laugh was genuine. His face beamed as he replied. "Ahh, you flatter me. But you must understand something. My art is simply an imitation." Moving his arm in a sweeping gesture over the meadow, he continued. "What you see in this meadow, that is the true masterpiece. Chamisa in autumn splendor. A sky so blue that even the Sangre de Cristo Mountains are humbled." Ed said nothing for a few moments. His gaze lingered over the meadow as if it was the first time he had ever seen it. "What we see here is the genuine masterpiece, Juanita. This is the masterpiece given to us from the hand of the Master."

Turning, he looked into Juanita's face. His eyes probing, he again spoke. "I am glad to see that you appreciate this loveliness." He smiled. "But, of course, I'm not at all surprised. My old friend, Brad Walker, a crusty old coot for sure, would never fall in love with a woman who was unable, or unwilling, to see the beauty of this world."

Ed's smile never left. But it also seemed to Juanita that his eyes never blinked. It was like something might happen that he could not possibly miss.

"Just by knowing Brad, I know a great deal about you." Ed pointed to Juanita's heart. "I can see things, Juanita. I can see things."

With a laugh exuding affection, Ed took Juanita by the arm. "Come on inside. Brad tells me he just wants to admire my art for a few minutes." Giving a wink, he continued. "I suspect you are being used as a diversion while that snake grabs a few of my most expensive pieces and sneaks them out the back door."

———

Mugs of tea and a plate of cookies were on the table when Juanita, Brad and Ed Romero took seats at a table in the back of Ed's art gallery. Juanita and Brad were seated side by side with Ed across from them. "Okay, my friends. All the doors are locked and a big closed sign has been placed on the entrance. That should be adequate to keep pests, vagabonds, and tourists out of our hair. My morning belongs to you." Looking at Brad, Ed made a statement that came across mostly as a question. "Judging from the tone of Brad's voice on the phone yesterday, I have a feeling that something troubling must be in the air. I'm very curious." Shifting his eyes from Brad to Juanita, Ed continued. "So, what's it going to be? Which one of you is going to tell me what it is that bothers you?"

When awkward silence was the only response from Juanita and Brad, another captivating smile came from across the table. "There is something going on here. I can tell that you are reluctant to talk about whatever it is you came here to talk about. Now, that is downright funny. You came here to talk, but now you are all buttoned up, apparently afraid to talk." Ed's voice was gentle. "You need to tell me why you have come here this morning. How can I help you?"

Looking across the table, Juanita's eyes betrayed amazement with both the humor and the insight coming from the artist. Pointing to Brad, her words were issued as a command. "He needs to begin."

"Your lady has spoken, Brad. Please, talk to me. I do not enjoy seeing you so troubled."

"Yes, Ed, as usual, you have nailed it. I'm not sure that the word *troubled* is exactly accurate. Juanita and I are confused and mystified about several things that have happened." Brad leaned forward. "I think it's fair to say that in addition to being confused and mystified, we are also a bit frightened."

"Sounds fascinating. But I'm not getting any younger as I sit here waiting on you to say what's on your mind. Let's get going."

With a final look of doubt cast in Juanita's direction, Brad began to speak. He began with the story of his becoming involved in an investigation that was a carryover from his days in the FBI. He told how a white extremist group had targeted a federal prosecutor and him in a campaign of revenge for their roles in the imprisonment of a member of their organization. Ed's face winced as Brad described how a blow to his head with a lead pipe had been intended to end his life.

Juanita looked to the ceiling as Brad continued. He described how a Mexican man with a huge mustache had rescued him after the attack. Brad recalled a painful journey on horseback to a frontier-style cabin. It was in this tiny cabin that a woman named Juanita, along with her brother, Manuel, had nursed him to health. Brad described a pungent broth that Juanita had prepared in a clay pot. He spoke softly when speaking of the miraculous relief it had delivered.

Ed Romero's scrutiny of Brad was unwavering. Juanita's eyes shifted between the two men.

An uncomfortable shifting of posture accompanied Brad's pause as he looked to Juanita. Returning his gaze to Romero, his next words were spoken with hesitation. "And then, Ed, I awakened in a modern hospital in Taos. I was told that I had been under a physician's care, here in the Taos hospital, for hours."

All sat quietly for a moment. Ed made no attempt to express or interject his thoughts.

With a look of a child about to confess stealing cookies, Brad gave a weak grin. "But Ed, there is just a little bit more."

With a lifting of eyebrows and a hint of a nod, Ed signaled for Brad to continue.

Brad's voice wavered as he again spoke. "The woman in the cabin. The woman who healed me. The woman who gave me broth." Brad looked to Juanita with a nod of his head. "It was this Juanita right here, Ed. The woman that I am desperately in love with. The woman I intend to share life with until I die. The Juanita at this table with us at this moment. They are one and the same, Ed. They are one and the same."

Juanita closed her eyes. Moisture glistened.

"The two of you have talked about this, I hope." Ed Romero's question was gentle but probing.

Dabbing at her eyes with a napkin, Juanita nodded in the affirmative.

Leaning back into his chair, Brad answered. "Yes, Ed. We've talked about it a million times. But something else happened to me that I've never had the courage to talk about. At least not until yesterday."

A barely discernible nod was once again the only response from across the table.

"But before I tell you more of my story, I think you need to hear from Juanita. Someone paid her a visit a few days ago. It was a visit that has changed both our lives."

Shifting his gaze to Juanita, Ed spoke. "By all means. I have a feeling this is going to be a fascinating story."

Clearing her eyes, Juanita began to speak. Emotion sometimes crept into her voice, but her direct gaze into Ed Romero's face never faltered. As the story of her visitor unfolded, Juanita was uncertain if she witnessed doubt or amazement from the man listening to her story. But a change of some sort developing in his face was unmistakable. As Juanita concluded with how the woman had simply walked away, vanishing into a storm, silence settled around the table.

"And you have even more to tell?" Ed Romero spoke as he expectantly looked back to Brad.

Folding his hands together on the table, Brad leaned forward. "I have more to tell you and I have something to show you as well." Brad repeated the story of the man in a nursing home. He told it just as he had confided to Juanita the previous afternoon. When finished, he slid his cell phone across the table, the photograph of Manuel Lujan's letter displayed on the screen. "Take a look at that, Ed."

After reading in silence for several seconds, Brad's friend looked across the table. His dark eyes held a new and strange intensity. Eyes that had been wide with interest now narrowed into mere slits. "Is this all? Is there more?" Romero's voice was loaded with anticipation.

Juanita and Brad exchanged glances. Brad nodded for Juanita to speak.

"Yes, there is more we have to tell you. What comes next is perhaps the biggest mystery of all." Juanita inhaled. With breath sealed within her lungs, she composed her thoughts. "The very first time that I had ever heard of Brad's experiences with the man in a nursing home was yesterday afternoon. When he told me the story, we were seated in the Kit Carson Cemetery. We had just discovered a gravestone. It was nearly buried after Lord knows how many years in the ground. We were lucky to have found it." Juanita stopped talking and looked to the ceiling. "I don't know whether to tremble or cry."

Romero's face and body had become rigid. His seemingly never-ending smile vanished as his dark eyes fired like lasers across the table.

With hesitation in her voice, Juanita recited from memory the gravestone's inscription. She then slid her cell phone across the table. "That's it, Ed. That is what we found yesterday."

Ed Romero looked as if he had been hit by an avalanche. Staring at Juanita, he did not speak. His eyes again opening wide, he leaned his body toward Juanita. Grasping her hand, he stared into her face with an intensity bordering on ferocious.

Brad had ceased to exist. Romero's entire world was Juanita.

Clinging to Juanita's hand, he also held her eyes. Seconds dragged before he finally opened his mouth to speak. "You are Juanita Lujan. Oh, my God. You are the woman I have heard about my entire life."

It was now Juanita who froze. The air in the room crystallized. No one dared breathe. Any movement threatened to shatter the moment.

Juanita returned Romero's intensity. With the faintest of movement, but without speaking, she signaled that she needed answers.

Reluctantly releasing Juanita's hand and breathing a deep exhale, Ed Romero leaned back into his chair. He shifted his eyes to Brad with an expression like he was looking at his friend for the first time.

Heat seemed to radiate within the silence that came from across the table. Seconds dragged before Brad managed to ask the obvious question. "What the hell, Ed? What are you talking about?"

Tapping his fingers over the tabletop, Romero hesitated as he looked to the ceiling, lost in thought. After what seemed an eternity, he spoke. "We need to take a drive. I do indeed have things to say. It is now my turn to tell you a story. But my story cannot be told in this room. It must be told somewhere else." He rose from his chair. "You're driving, Brad. Come on, let's go." With the words curtly spoken, Ed Romero stood and marched to the doorway leading to Brad's truck.

With only a shrug to Juanita's questioning expression, Brad took Juanita's hand as they followed.

With Brad behind the wheel and Juanita beside him, Ed took the back seat. Pointing, he directed Brad. "This way, up the hill and then turn right."

Having no idea what his friend had in mind, Brad followed the instructions. Reaching the intersection with Kit Carson Road, he made a right turn. Brad knew the road well. It was the way through Taos Canyon, leading to Angel Fire Resort and Eagle Nest.

No conversation took place as Brad followed the twisting road out of Taos. Within minutes, they entered forested land. Glimpses of structures or signs of habitation were sporadic.

Romero leaned forward from the rear seat, bringing his face closer to Juanita and Brad. "Make a right at the dirt road coming up."

Within feet of leaving the highway, what Romero had called a dirt road quickly deteriorated. Ruts gouged the soil and overgrown vegetation left little more than a pathway. Brad slowed his truck to a crawl as they descended the steep grade. Trees grew in a tangled canopy, obscuring the sun. Dark shadows swallowed Brad's truck as it crept. Human activity was obviously a seldom seen, and probably unwelcome, intruder.

"Just a little bit further." The words came from the back seat as a means of encouragement. The growing reticence felt by Juanita and Brad was obvious. Despite years of friendship between Brad and the artist, his mysterious behavior was pushing limits.

The steep decline finally leveled out as an entirely different world suddenly appeared. A meadow of lush grass basked beneath brilliant sunshine. Aspen trees, with hints of gold in their leaves, sprinkled the expanse. Massive cottonwoods grew along the far side, outlining the banks of an arroyo. It was the familiar story of the Southwest. When monsoon rains visited, the arroyo carried thirst-quenching water to the aged trees. But the gift often came in terrifying floods of destruction, a part of nature's balance.

"See that stone outcropping up ahead, behind the clump of aspen trees?" Still leaning forward, Romero extended a finger to direct Brad. "Head over there."

Without comment, Brad followed the command and eased his

truck over the grassy terrain. As they slowly approached the area, monstrous stone formations came into clearer view. Boulders sprouted from the meadow's floor as if they had been planted.

"This is beautiful." Juanita looked to the back seat as she spoke.

A mysterious smile beneath his mustache was Romero's only acknowledgment of her comment. After a few more seconds, he spoke again. "Here. Right here is where I want you to stop."

A gentle tap of the brakes brought the truck to a halt.

Twisting their bodies to look into the back seat, Juanita and Brad waited, giving their passenger an opportunity to explain himself. With a smile, he spoke. "I am going to sit right here for a few minutes. I want you to walk to those aspen trees. Then go on beyond the boulders. I will be coming along behind you soon. But first, you need to be alone for a while."

"Ed, if I didn't know you and think the world of you, right about now, I would be telling you to go sit on a chili pepper."

Tossing his head back, Ed Romero laughed out loud. "If only you knew." He laughed again. "If I sat on a chili pepper every time someone tells me to sit on a chili pepper, there would be more chilis in my asshole than grow in all of the state of New Mexico."

Leaning forward again, he looked back and forth between Juanita and Brad. "Now go. This is important. Take your time. I'll see you soon."

---

"What in the world are we doing out here? I have not the slightest idea what your friend is talking about or what he thinks we are doing." Juanita whispered as if she feared Ed could hear her speak from over one hundred yards away. "The way he acted and what he said in those last few moments in his studio give me goose-bumps. It's like he was looking right through me. I have no clue what he saw, but he sure as heck became mighty fired up." Juanita turned her face to Brad. "I'm feeling a little bit excited, perplexed, and frightened. All at the same time."

"I wish I could help you understand what's going on, but I'm also lost." Brad stopped walking. "There is a reason why we are out here. There is something here that Ed wants us to see." Brad looked about the meadow, giving a shrug as he smiled. "Or maybe my friend has breathed too many paint fumes and lost his marbles."

As they entered the aspen grove, Juanita and Brad unconsciously reached for the other's hand. When viewed up close, the formations of stone loomed even larger than they had appeared when seen from a distance. It was now obvious that the meadow extended beyond the boulders, reaching to the cottonwoods that grew along the arroyo and the meadow's boundary.

Clearing the aspens and walking through the garden of stones, Brad moved slowly. He was fascinated with the boulders and wondered how they had come to exist in such a flat and open meadow. Juanita's grip on Brad's hand suddenly became fierce as she abruptly halted. Urgency radiated from Juanita's gripping hand. Looking to Juanita in alarm, he saw her pointing straight ahead.

It took less than a blink for Brad to realize the reason for Juanita's frantic grasp. He felt his own heart leap. In contrast to an atmosphere of steadfast strength within the boulders, a scene of disrepair and decay rose from the meadow's floor. Beneath the brilliant sunshine and openness of the meadow, the diminutive structure of a crumbling cabin stood in lonely solitude. Like an abandoned animal, the walls and windows of the small cabin seemed to cower. A pitiful plea for compassion seemed to exude from within the graying skeleton that had at one time been a home.

"Oh God, Brad! Oh God!" Juanita's words were a choked whisper. "This is it. I've been here before." Forcing her head to move, Juanita turned to look at Brad. "I have lived in that cabin."

Feeling that the ground beneath his feet swayed, Brad blinked his eyes and held his breath. Finally, he also whispered. "Holy Jesus!" Returning Juanita's gaze, he managed to speak. "This is the place where you took care of me. Mustache brought me here. This is where I first laid eyes on you."

Moving with a creeping cadence, Juanita and Brad moved forward. A cabin that had at one time held life, but now condemned to a purgatory of abandonment, stood in silence. With each step, their hearts pounded. The cabin waited.

The structure barely existed. Years—centuries—of weather, rodents, and deterioration had consumed the cabin as if it were a rotten fruit. The roof was mostly collapsed. Walls leaned in precarious angles, on the brink of collapse. Remnants of a door somehow remained suspended, but hung awkwardly, actually blocking the entrance.

Not daring to enter, Juanita and Brad stood in sunlight. Focusing their eyes to see within the shadowed interior was a slow process. After long moments, Juanita pointed to one end of the cabin. A ghost of a fireplace could be discerned. Where the roof had collapsed, stones of a crumbled chimney lay scattered about the dirt floor. "That was what I had for a kitchen. It was just a table. I carried water from somewhere. I don't remember where. I just recall the clay pots that I used. I remember huddling close to the fire for warmth."

Nodding his head toward an area opposite the kitchen, Brad spoke with reverence usually reserved for a cathedral. "My bed was right there. That is where you cared for me. You gave me broth from your kitchen."

Silence was the only sound. From the cabin's dusky shadows, the breath of phantoms stirred. Memories from another world fluttered.

"Was I correct? Is this the place?" Even though Ed spoke softly, his words still shattered the moment.

Turning to face Ed, who had approached from behind, Juanita took the needed steps to bring herself within inches of his face. "Ed, you have been Brad's friend for years. You are a marvelous artist and a good man. You have brought us here without explaining why. Now it is time for you to talk. What is the story you promised? I'm out of patience with mystics and mystery. Please, Ed, talk to me right now."

Looking over Juanita's shoulder, Romero's eyes went to Brad. An affirmative nod and serious face made it clear that Brad agreed with Juanita's assessment.

"Yes, Juanita, you are absolutely right. it is time for talk. You have every right to know why I brought you here." Lifting an arm to indicate a clump of nearby stones, he spoke. "Please, let's sit and be comfortable."

Once gathered in a semi-circle, Juanita and Brad sat with impatient expectancy. Jumbled images and emotions roiled. What they had just seen and felt while standing outside the cabin had been one unexplained phenomenon too many.

Lifting his hands, palms out, to indicate he understood their feelings, Ed Romero began to speak. "Please, my friends, I am just an artist. I'm an artist who has learned how to search for beauty in everyday life. I then imitate that beauty on canvas. I try to do so in a way that will bring joy to others." An emphatic tone entered his voice. "I am in no way some sort of shaman or a man with extraordinary powers. I do not sit around sipping tea with ghosts or have the ability to peer into shrouded mists of the future." Ed smiled. "But I do observe closely. I pay attention to people and the world around me. I remember lessons that have been taught and stories that have been told." He paused. "And I absolutely believe that as we pass through life, many things happen that defy explanation. Things that cause me to believe that sometimes forces or spirits that we cannot see or understand enter our lives."

Unblinking eyes from Juanita and Brad told Ed to continue.

"I believe with all of my heart that the past never really goes away." Conviction was in Ed's voice. "Especially here in Taos, the past simply plays hide-and-seek. When things are just right, and when we least expect it, faces and voices from the past jump out. Right in front of us. There are times when those voices and faces are welcomed like old friends. Other times they are shunned." Lowering his voice, Ed cautioned. "Sometimes we run away in fear."

Offering time for a response, Ed paused. Barely discernible nods were all that he received.

"Based upon what I have heard from both of you this morning, I am convinced that this is one of those times. I think the past has returned. I think voices and faces from the past have visited you."

Clouds drifted. Juanita and Brad said nothing. The cabin listened.

"My ancestors have lived in this area for as long as anyone

knows. My memory goes back as far as my great-grandmother. Both she and my grandmother lived to be one hundred years old." Ed's mustache was a part of his smile. "That's two centuries of history and stories that have been a part of my raising. They have shaped my life.

"The history of Taos is complicated." Ed gave a sarcastic chuckle. "As with much of history, how it is told depends on who is doing the telling. I don't know if you know about the Taos Revolt of 1847. This was shortly after the U.S. Government had taken control of the New Mexico Territory. People whose bloodlines originated in Spain and Mexico, along with Navajo, Apache, Ute, and other tribes, suddenly found themselves under the laws of white men. White men who were newcomers to the land. The new rulers had no under-standing of the history or culture of the societies they now governed."

In a solemn tone, Ed continued with his story. "My great-grand-mother was a young girl during this time. She lived in Taos. Her home was near the plaza. She and her family witnessed firsthand a period of terrible days when hatred, misunderstandings, and alcohol came together to form a black cloud that shadowed Taos for years. I am going to take you back to that time. It is important that you understand what happened in those days. I want you to know the things that my great-grandmother saw and heard."

Taking a long breath that he held as his eyes closed, Ed Romero's demeanor transformed. He became storyteller, a performer for an audience. His voice remained soft but dark eyes suddenly burned with intensity. Rhythmic movements of arms and hands worked in concert with voice, eyes, and face to enthrall his listeners. Juanita and Brad listened. They became enthralled. Under the hypnotic spell of a master storyteller, they were led into the tunnels of history.

"The nightmare began on a bitterly cold January night. A man named Charles Bent, New Mexico's territorial governor, was sleeping in his home. His wife, Ignacia, along with several guests, happened to be in the home on the fateful night. Josepha Jaramillo, the wife of Kit Carson, was one of the guests.

"The peaceful sleep that only a warm adobe and piñon fire can bring was shattered by a thunderous pounding on the door.

Drunken bellowing, mostly in Spanish, echoed through the village. Joining in the clamor, war-song chants from men of the Taos Pueblo filled the streets. What Governor Bent and his guests heard was nothing less than a chorus of terror.

"Charles Bent had tried to be a decent governor. He had helped bring medical supplies to the area. He had pleaded with his superiors for more support and attention to the new frontier. But Governor Bent now found himself shouting through the door of his home, trying to make his voice heard over the bedlam of a mob. After asking what they wanted, Governor Bent's blood chilled in terror. What he managed to hear over the screaming and chanting was that it was his head they wanted. Men, shrieking like savages, demanded his head and howled that they intended to take it."

His eyes brimming with emotion, Ed stood up. His entire body becoming a part of the story.

"Ignacia and Josepha quickly realized that deadly danger was battering on their door. Fear took their breath and panic burned their lungs. Using axes, shovels, and their bare hands, the women began a frantic dig for escape through one of the adobe walls. Their fingers bleeding and minds numb with dread, the women pleaded with Governor Bent to come and escape with them." A sad shake of the head preceded Ed Romero's next words. "It was not to be.

"Hoping to appease the mob in some manner, Governor Bent continued shouting what he thought were words of reason. Sadly, this was not the night for reason. Within the frantic sounds of digging, hurled curses, and murderous chants, Governor Bent detected a new sound. It was the sound of pure terror. Invaders were now on his roof. Clawing a way through soil and clay, the mob gouged an opening. Stars could now be seen through the roof of the governor's home. In a shrieking charge, masses of bodies descended into the house. The doorway was knocked from its support and leveled to the floor. More bodies poured into the home. Arrows flew. Musket charges deafened, and smoke choked the air."

The meadow was still. Juanita and Brad did not move. No breeze or calling of a bird could be detected.

"Governor Bent was scalped alive. But not yet satisfied, his attackers continued their rampage. Bent's body was mutilated until death mercifully took his soul. Ignacia and Josepha were spared. But a poor slave girl, who stood up to the attackers in an act of loyalty and bravery, was brutally murdered. Her life was taken for the crime of trying to protect others."

Reverent silence held for several moments. The horror of a night long past was again alive.

"What I have told you so far is well known history. Survivors and witnesses have described all that happened. Thousands of words and countless books have been written to record this dark time in the history of Taos. But I'm sure you are wondering what all of this has to do with why I brought you here this morning."

A simple look from Juanita and a questioning nod from Brad answered the question.

"The story I just told you is only the beginning of what happened during that sad time. Much more tragedy was yet to come. You see, after the awful events of the attack on Governor Bent's home, the people of Taos Pueblo and angry New Mexicans began an even more savage crusade. They set out to kill every white person who crossed their path. Raw emotions and cheap alcohol fueled the fires of murder. Shrieks of 'Kill the Gringos' echoed as mobs grew in size and fervor. Attacks spread in all directions, extending into countryside far beyond Taos. A killing frenzy ruled for miles. The horror lasted for days."

Romero's voice lowered. "Even children were slaughtered. If a child, no matter the parents, was seen to have fair-colored skin or light-colored hair, that innocent life was snuffed out."

Juanita closed her eyes. Folding her arms about her chest, she rocked her body in a gentle sway. Bowing her head, she leaned her body into Brad.

"And now, my friends, the reason we are here. Parents of mixed-race children were terrified. Safety for their families drove every thought, every action. Panic spread as the killings continued. Desperate mothers searched for ways to change the shade of skin or hair of their children." Pointing to the cabin, Ed spoke with reverence. "Word quickly spread that the occupants of this house,"

Manuel Lujan and his sister, Juanita, were skilled in the art of dyeing skin and hair to different shades."

A gasp came from Juanita. Brad did not move.

Looking directly at Juanita, Romero spoke softly. "Parents smuggled their children to this house. They hid their children in wagon beds or stuffed them inside sacks. If the children's bodies were small enough, they were tucked away beneath the dresses of their mother. Whatever they could do to get their loved ones to Juanita and Manuel, they did it. Juanita and Manuel worked day and night. Not a mother, father, or child was ever turned away. No one knows for sure how many children's lives were saved because of what happened inside the house that you have just discovered."

With no idea of anything that could be said, Juanita and Brad turned their eyes to the cabin.

"At some point in time, word of what Juanita and Manuel were doing made its way to one of the marauding throngs. In the dark of a freezing night, people crazy with hate came into this meadow and descended upon this very house. Very much like what had happened at the home of Governor Bent, hysterical people swarmed like vultures. They forced a way into the home of two people who had worked to save the lives of children. Juanita and Manuel Lujan were dragged from their home." Romero paused, nodding his head to a point at the meadow's border. His next words carried crushing emotion. "They were dragged over frozen ground to that arroyo. Their bodies were flung into the bottom. The last sounds they heard were the frenzied howls of human beings gone mad. While lying in the creek that had given them water for living, Juanita and Manuel were filled with arrows."

Romero took a breath.

Juanita and Brad turned and looked in the direction of where the savage deed had occurred.

No one spoke for several seconds. His voice scarcely more than a whisper, Romero continued. "Soldiers from Santa Fe finally ended the revolt in a massacre of fire and blood within the church at the Taos Pueblo. My great-grandmother knew everyone involved in the events of those days. She knew the murderers. She also knew the murdered. So many lives were lost. Things slowly calmed. When realization of the savagery finally settled and emotions calmed, the people of Taos wept for the memory of Juanita and Manuel. Bitter tears fell for what happened on that shameful night. Juanita and Manuel were buried with honor in the cemetery."

With a look that said they all shared a secret, Romero's next words were spoken with a smile. "You found their grave."

Leaning his body to be closer to Juanita and Brad, a sense of intimacy held the three people. "My great-grandmother grew into womanhood in Taos. The memories of what she saw and heard in those days was forever seared into her memory. Years later, she brought her children, my grandmother, to visit this place many times. She was passionate that the lessons of hatred must never be forgotten and never be repeated. The noble pilgrimage that my great-grandmother began has continued. As a small boy, my grandmother, along with my mother, brought me here. We spent time in this meadow and in that old house. They brought me here many times. They wanted me to see everything. They had me go inside the house. I have touched the windows. I have breathed the air within its walls." Ed turned. "I have stood over there." He pointed to the arroyo. "I have touched the soil that holds the blood of Juanita and Manuel. The story that I just told you has been repeated to me since I was a child. Everything we have seen and spoken about today is a valued part of who I am. It is in my heart and in my soul."

Shifting his eyes to Brad, Romero continued. "And Brad, let me tell you about the man who you saw in your dreams. The man with the big mustache."

"I'm listening, Ed."

"There was a man in Taos during this time. He was known to the locals only as Mustache. He was the child of parents who left Mexico to settle in Taos. He became somewhat of a legend because of the huge mustache he always wore and carefully groomed. He married a woman from the Taos Pueblo, and because of this, Mustache was accepted in both worlds. Months after the killings, it was learned that Mustache had helped many parents smuggle their children to Juanita and Manuel. He became a local hero for his bravery. After listening to your stories, I am certain that it was Mustache who rescued you and delivered you on horseback to this very house."

It was Ed's happy smile that next appeared. "So now, my dear friends, I hope you understand why I brought you here."

"Oh, my God," Juanita whispered. "I had no idea. All I know to say is thank you."

"You don't need to thank me. I am the one to be grateful. Because you came to me, I have been blessed to be a part of an experience that I never dreamed would come to me. It is I," Romero pointed to his heart, "who is blessed and filled with gratitude."

Lifting his hand into the air, Ed indicated that he was not yet finished. "But there is more. There is one more thing that you should know." He began pacing slowly. "For years after the murders, and to this very day, people swear that sometimes at night, lights of a lantern can be seen burning within the old cabin. Many of my fellow citizens of Taos tell me that they have seen this miracle. I believe them. Practically every person who has been raised in Taos accepts without question that the spirits of Juanita and Manuel still visit this meadow." A fierce expression and a jabbing finger emphasized his words. "I want you to know something. I believe with all my heart and soul that the spirits of Juanita and Manuel are still with us. I also believe that restless forces continue to haunt this place. I believe that, for whatever reason, those forces sometimes choose to illuminate Juanita's old home. A light still shines there. It shines for those who lost everything."

Ed Romero cast his eyes to the sky. "And I swear before all of heaven, I have believed in Juanita and Manuel Lujan all of my life. And now, I find myself sitting here with you. God has given me the honor of actually meeting Juanita Lujan." Romero shifted his focus to Brad. "And, Brad, what God has planned for you, I have no idea. After learning of your experience, there is no doubt that you met and talked with Manuel Lujan. He was the man who spoke with you from a nursing home bed. Someone far beyond this beautiful meadow and simple cabin has touched you. Never stop listening, Brad. Never stop listening."

As he spoke, Romero's mustache and white teeth again blended as one into a smile. "And now, Brad, you share love with this woman. What a miracle. I certainly do not understand everything, but I promise you, the hand of God is at work here."

Peaceful silence of the meadow was welcomed. There was nothing appropriate to say. Juanita leaned into Brad as he placed an arm about her shoulders. Ed and Brad both looked upward as if the New Mexico sky held answers.

"I want to see where it happened." Juanita's determined proclamation brought an end to the silence. She abruptly stood. "Take me to the arroyo. I want to see for myself."

Without responding, Ed and Brad also stood. With a tentative look to Juanita, Romero contemplated the request before giving a slow movement of his head. "If you are sure that is what you want, Juanita, let's go." He began walking.

Nothing was said as they walked toward the arroyo. The narrow chasm remained out of sight until they stood at its edge. Separating the meadow from a steep hill and dense forest, the ravine had been gouged by a small stream that now merely trickled. Standing on the precipice, three sets of eyes peered into the miniature canyon. The soothing sound of water rippling over stone was idyllic.

"Is this the place?" Her eyes never leaving the depths of the arroyo, Juanita whispered her question.

"No. We are close, but this is not the place." Romero turned to face the cabin. "The pathway is now overgrown, but when I was young, it was easily seen. In the old days, when people lived in the cabin. . ." Romero halted his speech. "When you lived in the cabin, Juanita, you followed the pathway to the creek for your water supply. It is much too steep here at this point. Follow me and I will show you the only place where a person could walk to the stream."

Once again, Juanita and Brad followed in silence. Walking downstream, they traversed the edge of the arroyo's nearly vertical walls. Romero stopped and pointed toward the cabin. "Okay, from this angle, you can see a faint outline that once was the pathway from the cabin to the stream."

Lifting hands to shade their eyes, Juanita and Brad squinted into the sun. Both nodded that they could see.

"Follow the pathway. It leads to a gentle slope that leads right down to the water."

"I see it." Juanita spoke.

"In the old days, that was the only place that could be used as a crossing for horses and wagons."

"Is that where it happened?" Juanita's voice was determined.

A tentative nod was the affirmative reply.

Juanita now took the lead. She walked with purpose and without speaking.

Upon reaching the point identified by Romero, Juanita halted. Looking down, she peered into the creek's bottom. Rounded smooth through centuries of nature's relentless flow, the creek's bed of stones shimmered beneath crystal clear water.

Juanita turned to face the old cabin. No one spoke. Ed and Brad stood behind Juanita, neither knowing what to expect. Brad was not certain that Juanita was even breathing.

"Show me." Juanita's brown eyes looked to be drowning in sorrow. But a fierce blaze also fired. "Show me exactly."

Gently stepping around Juanita, Ed approached the water's edge. He pointed. "Right here, Juanita. It was right here where the water curves to the right. My mother and grandmother brought me here. They said it was important for me to see this place. They wanted me to feel what happened."

Juanita stared into the water.

"On that horrible night, it was winter. The stream was ice. Water never moved their bodies after death." Romero was quiet, closely watching Juanita before continuing. "Juanita and Manuel died together. This is the place. They were embracing as the arrows pierced their bodies. That is how they died. That is how they were found."

Stepping away, Romero made room for Juanita to access the hallowed ground of her history. She took his place. She stood on the ground where Juanita Lujan had perished. Dropping to her knees, Juanita appeared to be in prayer. Dipping her hand into the creek, she was silent as water touched her skin. Searching for healing in the gentle flow, Juanita felt the power of water. Clear and cold. Hopefully cleansing.

Brad felt his heart was about to burst. Romero's hand found a way to Brad's shoulder. A solid grip conveyed support to his friend. Juanita remained on her knees, her back to the men and face hidden. There was nothing to say. Within the endless flow of a small creek, time and memories made their journey.

Standing again, Juanita turned to face the men. Her eyes moist, she spoke. "Thank you, Ed. Thank you for what you have taught us today. Thank you for bringing us to the cabin. And thank you most of all for bringing me here. I don't know when or how I am going to process all of this." She gave a faint smile. "But I absolutely know how lucky I am to have both of you wonderful men in my life." Juanita moved into Brad's arms for an intense embrace. "Enough already." Juanita smiled as she stepped away from Brad. "This has been quite the day. It's time for me to be a big girl. I have to figure things out and find myself." Juanita moved to Ed, lifted her hand and touched his cheek. "And it is time for us to leave you alone so that you can get back to creating more of your incredible art."

"I already know what my next painting will be. I'm going to paint this meadow and your cabin. When I finish, it will be yours."

"That will be marvelous. Thank you."

With the somber mood now beginning to lighten, Ed surveyed their surroundings and began to talk. "On a beautiful autumn day such as this, with the creek barely flowing, it is easy to underestimate how quickly things can change. It is not always this tranquil. When rains come, water flows through this arroyo in torrents. I've seen the creek rise until water reaches the meadow. It is something to see." Pointing to where Juanita had previously knelt, he continued. "Notice how the creek juts abruptly to the right. With only a little bit of rain, that sharp bend traps debris under the surface. The water becomes a monstrous swirl with tremendous power. It is a frightening sight."

"What is that over there?" Brad pointed across the arroyo to a mound of tree trunks that had obviously been trimmed and deliberately stacked.

With a sarcastic chuckle, Ed grinned. "Our tax dollars at work.

That is all New Mexico state land. A few years ago, a beetle infestation came through and killed a bunch of trees. The state began a process of clearing and cleaning to reduce fire danger. After a few weeks of work, some environmental groups got their hair singed because of too many roads being cut into the forest. They said the trees were already dead and should be left standing to let Mother Nature do her work. They claimed that some species of endangered birds needed the dead trees for nesting." Romero laughed. "So that big pile of tree trunks will remain right there until a judge in Santa Fe makes a decision."

"Got ya." Brad began walking back toward his vehicle. "I have no idea who is right or wrong. But you can go to the bank that an army of lawyers will make a ton of money no matter which way it goes."

Walking quietly, they covered the distance to Brad's truck. In lingering moments, they took a final look over the meadow. Emotions in turmoil, Juanita and Brad said a silent farewell as they departed.

# NINE

Hey you two

I've been thinking of you a ton and hoping you have had time for a little fun stuff to help forget the nightmare you experienced.

Here is the latest on Luther Birdwell.

If anyone knows where he is they aren't talking. Friends, family, associates, and known hangouts have been canvassed but no solid leads so far.

What has been learned is that he is running with a long-time friend named Boone Curtis. No surprise, but Curtis also has a history of wildlife law violations.

He was convicted, fined and sentenced to one year in prison in Colorado for illegally capturing mountain lions. He would cripple the lion by shooting it in the foot or stomach so that high-paying clients of his so-called outfitting and guide service could easily track and kill the animal.

Four months ago, Birdwell and Curtis were involved in a traffic accident in Albuquerque. Curtis was the driver and Birdwell the passenger. The other party was at fault, so no charges were filed.

There are no warrants currently outstanding for Curtis. Birdwell has an ex-wife in Utah who hates him with a passion. She has told investigators that Birdwell and Curtis are lifelong friends and will always make money by means of illegal hunting or trapping.

At this time, we have no idea of where the two men might be. Lots of state and federal people are working hard to find them.

I just wanted to keep you in the loop.

Take your time in deciding when to come back to the Albuquerque rat race.

Juanita, everyone in the office asks about you daily. Every time I walk past your empty desk, I miss you terribly.

So long for now and please stay in touch.

Margaritas and lazy days to you both!

Janice

THE TEXT MESSAGE was read in silence following simultaneous vibrating of their phones.

"What do you make of that?" Juanita sipped a coffee and looked across the cab of Brad's truck. Grinning, she issued a command. "In the name of heaven, pull over and park. Please don't kill us both over that greasy donut you are so obsessed with."

Attempting to drive, drink coffee, and devour a donut, all while reading Janice's text was proving to be a challenge for Brad. "I think your friend, Janice, is just another typical female lawyer. She should know that this is my coffee time and not bother me for at least another hour. I'm going to have a talk with that woman next time I see her."

"Poor bambino." Juanita's laugh filled the truck's cab.

Juanita's laugh always had a magical effect on Brad. Now, as she delighted in poking fun at his grumbling, Brad realized that he could not remember the last time he had heard her truly laugh. Glancing between the road ahead and the laughing woman beside him, he passed his coffee mug to Juanita. "Please hold this for me and try not to spill. While you laugh your little brown buns off, I'll park this beast so we can talk."

After managing to pull onto a wide shoulder of the road and park, Brad turned to face Juanita full on. "We can talk about the text message, but only after something much more important."

"And what might that be?"

"That something might be a coffee-flavored kiss with a hint of donut glaze."

Juanita's beautiful laugh again filled the cab and delivered a sense of peace that Brad had not felt in days. Leaning toward each other across the cab, Brad's request was granted, but only for a peck. Pulling away, Juanita winked as she returned his coffee mug. "Don't get anything started here, you horny coot. You are the one who insisted on going fishing this morning. Don't be blaming women or lawyers for your troubles."

Easing back to his side of the truck, Brad sipped coffee and was quiet.

Face and eyes smiling, Juanita said nothing. She patiently watched as Brad contemplated a response.

"Yep, I'm the one who wanted to fish. I really need something to get my mind off the past few days and all the craziness that has happened. Time on a trout stream with my fly rod. That is the best medicine I can ever have for just about anything." With a quick afterthought, Brad spoke again. "And time with you, of course."

"I understand and am thrilled we are doing this. This will be good for both of us." Juanita touched Brad's hand. "I don't care if we stay for an hour or spend all day on the water. Today belongs to us."

"I hear what you say." Brad pointed to the cell phone lying in his lap. "But the message from Janice is a reminder that some things don't take a day off just because we want to forget about them for a while. Somebody somewhere, and who knows when, will end up face to face with those two jerks. That will be an arrest where a mistake could be deadly." Following a somber pause, Brad concluded. "After our encounter with Birdwell, we sure don't need to be reminded of that."

Mirth had left Juanita's eyes. "What do you think? Where have they gone? Where are they holing up?"

Hiking his shoulders, Brad sighed. "Who the heck knows. My guess is that they have friends who will put them up for a while. Could be in the middle of a big city or a cabin in the middle of nowhere. But after a while, those arrangements don't suit a lifestyle. That's when people like Birdwell begin to sneak back out into the world." Brad gave another shrug. "And that's when a routine traffic stop or some sort of slipup can dearly cost a police officer."

Quietly sipping their coffee, Juanita and Brad drifted into their own thoughts. Their drive north on New Mexico Highway 522 placed them at the foot of the Sangre de Cristo Mountains. Early morning light was soft on the aged giants rising above the desert floor. To the west, the valley of the Rio Grande River stretched to infinity. San Antonio Mountain was a mere silhouette on the horizon.

"I love this." Juanita cradled her coffee in both hands. "We are doing exactly the right thing by coming here. We need a day to calm our souls." Juanita again reached to touch Brad's hand. "Let's get to the river. I want to breathe the air, listen to the water, all that back-to-nature stuff. And who knows? I suppose it's remotely possible that there may be a trout, an itty bitty baby trout, foolish enough to let you think you know how to cast."

Pulling back onto the highway, Brad reached for the radio knob. "I prefer music, even if it's bad music, over your insults."

---

A sprinkling of forest service campgrounds were occupied as Juanita and Brad entered the canyon. Once past the camping areas, no signs of humanity interfered with the day of solitude and beauty they both yearned to enjoy. After parking, Juanita and Brad walked to the water. Carrying only one rod, they took turns casting as they leisurely waded upstream. Aspen leaves, showing hints of gold, shimmered in the higher ridges. Cottonwoods blazed along the river's banks. When the sun hung directly over their heads, a streamside lunch of apples, cheese, and water was more delectable than food from a five-star restaurant.

"This has been a perfect morning." Juanita sighed. "Exactly what we needed."

"You are so right. I learned about the healing nature of a trout stream long ago. When I step into the water, it is like greeting an old friend that I have been missing. But just as importantly, stepping into the water helps to leave troubles behind. While standing in the water today, with you by my side, not a single thought of Luther Birdwell has entered my mind. Old Luther gets left behind when I step into that stream."

"I've never thought about fishing exactly like that. But you are absolutely right. Today has been a balm for my soul."

"You're up." Brad eased his body against a boulder. I'm going to stay right here and soak up more of this sunshine. Your casting technique needs a bit of expert critique. I'm the man for the job. Try not to embarrass yourself."

Without a word, Juanita reached for the fly rod. Stepping into the water, she mumbled, "Watch this, smart ass." After a few steps into the stream, she fired a daggered glance to Brad and began to cast. For the millionth time, Brad fell in love. Like a living sculpture, her brown skin, black ponytail, and slender arms became one with the fly rod. In a mixture of pride and envy, Brad watched. With each cast, her line looped perfectly before streaking forward. In a final arc of poetic grace, the fly touched the water with the softness of a shadow.

"You know, young lady, I've been fly fishing for years. My partners have always been grizzled old goats with stringy hair and ugly whiskers. But the way you fill out those waders. . ." Brad left his thought unfinished for a moment. "For the first time ever, I'm thinking of something other than fishing."

Stooping to dip her hand into the stream, Juanita made a direct hit onto Brad's face with a splash of cold water. As if Brad did not even exist, Juanita continued casting, maintaining focus on her rod and the water. Without so much as even turning to look at Brad, she called out over shoulder. "Pay attention, you dirty old man. You might learn something."

———

Angled light from a sinking sun illuminated canyon walls as Juanita and Brad began the journey home. Reminiscing on the magic of their day and the beauty of autumn, they drove past the camping grounds at the mouth of the canyon. Absorbed in the moment, neither of them noticed the bright red pickup truck deliberately tucked deep within an overhang of trees. They did not see the astonished look or the bandages covering the face of the man standing beside the pickup truck. They did not see the hatred in his stare as he watched the dust trailing Brad's truck.

# TEN

"Boone! Boone! Get your ass out of the tent and come over here." Luther Birdwell's eyes remained focused on the settling dust as Boone Curtis emerged from the tent where he had been napping. Yawning and massaging the bristles of a neglected beard, Curtis sauntered to where Birdwell stood.

"What the hell you yelling about? Sounds like your balls are on fire." Curtis looked around their camping area. "I don't see no fire and don't smell no smoke." Lifting a leg, a low rumble came from the backside of his trousers. "What the hell, a chipmunk bite you on the pecker?"

"Look at that." Birdwell pointed to remnants of dust still suspended in the air. "Who do you think just drove down that road?" Not waiting for a response, Birdwell snarled his next words. "It was them sorry-ass bastards that drove right past me." Birdwell turned his head to spit.

"You ain't making a whole lot of sense, Luther. Maybe you got that bandage wrapped too tight? Might be your brain needs a little more air." Curtis lifted a leg again. "How bout you start talking like a normal person. If I want crazy talk, all I need is a wife or a whore."

Curtis grinned. "I had a wife once and I ain't going down that road again. Now, you going to say what the hell is wrong?"

Turning to face Curtis, Birdwell's eyes glared. "I'll tell you what's wrong. While your lazy ass is snoozing away in the tent, I come over here by the trees to take a piss. Just as I'm getting all tucked in and zipped, I hear a vehicle coming down the road. Me being a neighborly sort of guy, I plan to give a friendly wave to our visitors." Birdwell stopped talking and shook his head in disbelief. Once again, he turned to silently stare at the empty road and said nothing more.

"Luther, I ain't getting no younger and it's gonna be dark soon. Wanna tell me what or who you saw that's eating your ass so bad?"

Glaring at his partner, Birdwell hurled words like bullets. "The reason me and you are stuck here in this God-forsaken place is who just drove down that road. The reason half the cops in the country are looking to lock my ass up in a cage is who just drove by. The reason me and you ain't in Taos tonight drinking whiskey and finding ourselves some pussy just drove by." Birdwell pointed to the road. "Get the damned picture? Both of them twat-faced bastards just passed within a hundred feet. Cruising along, happy as can be." Birdwell flung another spit.

Expression on the face of Boone Curtis transformed. Drawing his shoulders back, his eyes narrowed into slits. "You sayin what I think you're sayin?"

"That's exactly what I'm saying." Birdwell continued searching the road as if he expected the vehicle to reappear. "The goofy son of a bitch that was trying to save that deer and his little chili pepper squeeze from the gift shop, they just drove past us. They drove right damned past us."

Both men now stared down the road.

"Did they see you?"

Shaking his head, Birdwell muttered, "No, they never even looked over here in this direction. No problem there."

Curtis hesitated before speaking. "You're pretty damned hard to miss, Luther. You got so much white shit wrapped around your head, somebody might think you're one of them mummies from Egypt, Africa, or wherever the hell those fuckers is buried."

"No, dammit. I told you. They didn't even glance my way. I'm certain."

Nothing was said as Birdwell and Curtis processed what had just happened. Birdwell broke the silence. "I reckon we might as well go ahead and have a talk right now. I've been putting it off but now is as good a time as it's ever going to be."

"You are wound up mighty tight. You've been wound ever since you got your eyeballs scratched to hell. Now what's this you wanna talk about?"

"Been doing some thinking, Boone. The hard kind of thinking. I've made up my mind. I know damned well what needs to be done and I aim to do it."

Folding his arms over his chest, Boone evaluated his partner. "Okay. Care to tell me something about whatever the hell this big decision is all about?"

Leveling his eyes directly onto the face of his partner, and with a voice as calm as if he was ordering a sandwich, Birdwell spoke. "I'm going to kill them. I'm going to murder both of those bastards. I'm going to kill them and then stomp on their heads till their brains squirt out."

Curtis remained quiet. His eyes narrowed as he spoke. "You're serious, aren't you? You are standing there, serious as hell in July, and talking about killing a couple of people. What's gone wrong with you? You think you're just gonna casually kill a couple of folks, then drive off, have pie and ice cream and live happy ever after?"

"You bet your ass, I'm serious. I'm as serious as I've ever been about anything."

"Think maybe we oughta talk about this, Luther? You need to remember something. It's thanks to your genius idea of trying to figure a way to get a little money for that damned Injun pot that started this whole mess anyway. You wasn't thinking then and you ain't thinking now."

"We're talking more than a little money. That pot is worth a fortune. I just don't know the best way to collect." Birdwell spit. "But I gotta admit you are partway right. I should never have traded pottery for an elk head. I let that fat Texan screw me."

"I told you when you did it that you was a damned fool. That shit ain't nothin but Injun Tupperware. Now look at the fix we're in." Curtis glared at Birdwell. "Both our phones been buzzing like pissed off rattlesnakes all day. Looks like every damned cop in the country is out looking for you. I call that being in a fucking fix."

"What's done is done. I'm a wanted man. I've got a warrant for murder over my head and it ain't going away." Birdwell's voice became hard. "We've talked about this, Boone. We were together the night we whacked Ranger Rick. Nobody knows or cares which one of us fired the arrow. We were together and that makes both of us guilty. No judge or jury gives a rat's ass about who did what that night. We were together and once we're caught, we're going down together."

Curtis was quiet.

"The reason we are in this pickle barrel is because I fucked up and didn't kill that Bambi-loving shitbird when I had his ass in the creek."

Eyes locked, Birdwell and Curtis evaluated each other and their situation.

Birdwell continued. "Now, you tell me something, Mr. Einstein. What's the difference in facing the murder of a single game warden or the murder of a game warden along with a couple of pussy-footed lovebirds? It's all the same bowl of shit salad, Boone. All the same."

Curtis made no reply. He continued to stare. Eyes of iron evaluated the man he had been running with for years.

"It's the same jail cell, Boone! It's the same electric chair, the same needle. The same gas chamber. Whatever some damned fancy lawyers and a judge in a big-ass robe decide, everything is the same for me and you. Either way, we are just as locked up or just as dead."

Birdwell sucked hard and held his breath. "We've been in prison, Boone. And we both have swore to God that we will never go back."

Curtis refused to speak or to take his eyes from Birdwell.

"Let me tell you something, Boone. It was a damned woman who sent me to prison. It was a woman. She damned near shot my ass. Then she gets all dressed up, just looking pretty as a picture. She sat up on a big old chair in a courtroom, legs crossed all prim and proper." Birdwell snarled. "And with her sweet little sing-song voice, she told a judge and a jury what a bad man I was. She said that I was mean cause I didn't talk to the animals and sing with the birds. Kiss my ass."

Hurling another spit, Birdwell glared at Curtis. "Every night I spent in my cell, I had wonderful dreams about going back to Utah and giving her what she deserves. I never did do it and that has been one huge mistake. A mistake that I fully intend to correct."

"You've been a free man all this time. Maybe not going back to Utah was a good idea. Where would you be today if you had gone back and found the broad? What's all of a sudden become so different now?"

"There is one thing that is different, Boone." Jabbing a finger into the chest of his partner, Birdwell hissed his next words. "When our asses are rotting in a cell or they shoot us full of nighty-night juice, we can damn well walk into hell knowing that them two love birds are feeding worms in New Mexico. I refuse to rot away in a cell or go to my grave knowing them two sweeties are out having Sunday picnics. You think I'm going to rot in jail while they live the good life? Kiss my ass. Ain't gonna happen, Boone. It ain't gonna happen."

Processing Birdwell's rant, Curtis remained stoic. He faced his companion without moving.

Birdwell's chest heaved as if he had just completed a marathon.

"Sounds to me like you're giving up." Curtis finally spoke. "What about running? You're right about prison. Not exactly my idea of a good time."

"Run? Run where for Christ's sake? Sure, me and you know how to live off the land. We can go up to Montana and live in a damned cave or a hole in the ground for a while. But someday we gotta go to a store. We have to have ourselves some sort of supplies. In winter, it might be nice to have a coat or some gloves. Personally, I don't see much difference between that kind of survival and living in a nice warm prison."

Silence and a stare from Curtis.

"Come on, Boone. Use your head. We've known all along that it could end like this. The night we put an arrow through that fucking ranger changed everything. Nobody really gives a shit about a few rich fuckers paying us good money so they can hang an elk or deer head in their fancy house." Shaking his head, Birdwell spoke with resignation. "But folks tend to get upset when some damned cop goes down. Me and you are gonna be hunted like dogs for as long as we live."

"I can see that you been thinking about this a spell."

"Come on, Boone! Hell yes, I've been thinking. Maybe it's time you started thinking. How long do you plan to sit here in this campsite, hiding like a scared rabbit? The party is over! We are in big-time trouble. I'm willing to run for as long as we can. I sure as hell vote to give them-bounty hunting boy scouts a run for their money." Birdwell's breath came in ferocious gasps. "But, by God, when the day comes that I get locked up, it's gonna be for a lot more than getting rid of one little animal-loving fucker with a badge. I plan to kill the two people that I should have killed in the creek. Then, I'm taking my ass to Utah. I'm gonna find that ranger cunt and give her a ticket to the happy hunting ground." Birdwell shrugged. "After that, let the manhunt begin. Hell, I'm even thinking it might be kinda fun to read about myself in the paper every day."

A slow nod came from Curtis. "I guess what you're saying is this. Either we go down together, in a blaze of glory as they say, or we say adios."

With a slow, thoughtful shake of his head, Birdwell answered. "Yep, Boone, I reckon you're right. That's the way it's gotta be. We finish things up together, get famous and raise hell, or we take a different road." Following a spit, Birdwell looked to Curtis and waited.

"Okay, Luther." Choosing each word slowly and deliberately, Curtis spoke his decision. "We'll have it your way. As far as we know, ain't no warrant for me. That won't be the case for very long. I'll go into town tomorrow and keep an eye on that shop where you took the Injun pot. If they're around, I'll find 'em and let you know." Curtis turned and walked to the tent.

Leaning against the truck, breath still heaving, Birdwell crossed his arms over his chest. Trying to calm his mind, he ran his eyes over the surrounding canyon walls and forest. In the quiet of the evening, a sound registered. "Well, I'll be go to hell." Looking up, he whispered to himself. Cautiously shifting his body, Birdwell opened the back door of the pickup truck. In practiced slow motion of silence and stealth, he wrapped his fingers around the shotgun lying in the seat. Bringing the weapon to his shoulder, he released the safety mechanism. Leveling the bead of the barrel on the top branch of a ponderosa pine, Birdwell held his breath. Gentle pressure. Trigger snapped. Detonation. Steel pellets discharged. From canyon wall to canyon wall, the haunting sound rolled like thunder.

A smile of satisfaction twisted Birdwell's face as he walked to the base of the tree. Wedging the toe of his boot beneath the mangled and bloody creature, he gave a violent kick. Against an evening sky, the owl appeared to be in flight. The dead bird then plummeted. With a sickening thud, the river accepted the body, taking it to wherever rivers flow.

Returning the shotgun to the truck, Birdwell muttered. "Hoot your way to hell, you little feathered bastard."

# ELEVEN

Lifting the pot to eye level, Melissa Tafoya squinted her eyes. "This is Acoma, I'm certain. It matches the potter's symbol etched on the bottom and the design is correct. This potter has been dead for some time, but I am confident it is genuine. I can't say exactly, but I have no doubt that this is quite valuable. Many thousands is my guess." Turning the pot within her hands, her voice carried reverence as she spoke. "When you brought the photograph of this treasure to my gallery in Santa Fe, I knew I just had to drive up here to see it in person." Melissa winked at Foster. "And of course, sneaking a cup or two of your coffee and giving you grief is always fun."

"I'm on to you, Melissa." Foster grinned. "Your true colors are as easy to see as a palm tree in the Arctic."

Once again admiring the pot, Melissa continued. "When these rare pieces come into my gallery, I never cease to marvel. I think they are sacred."

Juanita, Foster, and Brad sat on the front porch of Foster's shop. The turquoise and silver necklace draped about Melissa's throat captured warmth of the late morning sun. The beauty of what she wore enhanced the serenity of the day. Adjusting the pot to see it from different angles, she continued. "No matter the origin or design, the images chosen by the artist of such pieces are the stories of life." Melissa smiled at her audience. "I swear, there are times when I honestly think I can hear the voices of the people or smell the smoke of the fires that shaped these magnificent creations."

Foster rocked his chair gently. "Well, you know the bizarre circumstances of how this came into my possession. I sure can't try to sell it. That would be wrong on many levels. I would love your suggestion on what is the best thing to do."

Silver hair contrasting against her brown skin served to emphasize Melissa's persona of elegance and professional expertise. Decorative reading glasses perched on the bridge of her nose hinted of the sassiness and humor that had made her and her gallery a Santa Fe icon.

"My first suggestion is that you give this magnificent pottery to me as a gift. You should do this because I am such a wonderful person." Melissa peered over glasses. "And because I will burn your gift store to the ground if you fail to do as I wish."

Throwing his head back in a laugh, Foster replied, "I've been told you are the big boss of Santa Fe's Mafia. You certainly carry the look of a knee-breaker." Turning to Juanita and Brad, he forced a serious tone. "For heaven's sake, right here sits an FBI guy and a big-time criminal prosecutor. Isn't there something illegal in what this lady just said? Surely it qualifies as extortion, racketeering, or criminal bullying." Foster grinned. "Or criminal bullshit."

Lifting his arms in mock surrender, Brad spoke. "There is no way this lady could be taken into custody by a solitary agent. Don't look at me."

"The jury finds the defendant innocent of all charges." Juanita spoke with authority as she looked directly to Melissa. "You are free to go, Ms. Tafoya. All court costs will be the responsibility of the man who brought these frivolous charges against you."

"Oh my, this day is starting off beautifully." Melissa smiled as she gingerly returned the pottery to Foster. "Since no one can speak to how that creep happened to have possession of the pot, I think you must be careful. It is either stolen property or in some manner involved in nefarious dealings." Melissa looked to Foster. "That means naughty stuff."

Juanita and Brad smiled as Foster rolled his eyes.

Melissa was thoughtful for a moment. "I'll tell you what, Foster. For another cup of your wonderful piñon coffee, I will give you a name and contact info for the director of the Indian Pueblo Cultural Center in Albuquerque. The director and all of the wonderful people who manage the center are friends of mine. I will tell them to expect your call. I think they are the perfect experts for something like this."

"Sounds great to me. Thank you, Melissa. I've been struggling with what to do." Casting a dubious look to Juanita and Brad, Foster stood. "It's a cinch that these two so-called hotshots haven't come up with any ideas. Now, I'm going to return this baby to the safe. Then, I'll bring that coffee you desire." Holding the pottery with the care of a newborn infant, Foster stepped through the doorway into his gift store.

"I love that man." Melissa smiled. "We've been friends from way back in the olden days." Once again peering over her glasses she smiled. "You know what I mean? Those olden days of long ago when we were young students together the University of New Mexico."

"He is a jewel for sure." Juanita returned Melissa's smile. "Have you ever met his brother, my Uncle Ernie? Talk about a character. And when the two of them are together, oh my goodness, it is an absolute circus."

"Circus is an understatement. One of my favorite college memories involves those two clowns." Melissa threw her hands into the air. "Ernie, Foster, and another friend of theirs were all on campus for a Halloween party. They dressed up as the Three Stooges. Their impressions were spot on. And then they surprised everyone by giving a pretty darned good concert of country music. Moe, Larry, and Curly singing 'Rawhide' and 'Red River Valley' was hilarious. But honestly, they were very talented vocalists."

"What you kids talking about?" Foster stepped onto the porch carrying coffee for Melissa and himself. With a dismissive tone and a curt jerk of his head, he spoke. "Juanita and Brad, go get your own. I serve only responsible adults in this establishment."

"I will do just that, Uncle Foster." Juanita headed for the doorway. "And don't you worry about the topic of our conversation. I promise, it had nothing to do with responsible adults."

———

No one paid attention to the unkempt man sitting on the outdoor patio of the coffee shop across the street. Keeping a coffee mug close to his face, the icy stare he directed toward the people conversing on the porch of a gift store went unnoticed.

# TWELVE

Good day and the latest update for you.

Once we found out about Boone Curtis we re-examined the partial prints recovered. From beer cans and the arrow at the murder scene.

Bingo! Boone Curtis was at the murder scene and a warrant will be issued later today.

Still no leads on where either of them are currently located. Everyone is betting that they are together but laying low.

An anonymous tip was received in Utah that both Birdwell and Curtis have set up a camp in remote mountains east of Salt Lake City. That is rugged country and is also becoming crowded with hunters.

Since the tip was anonymous, there is no way to validate the legitimacy of the information, but Utah is a likely place for them to hide. General consensus is that Birdwell and Curtis are hiding out together and probably receiving help from friends. Beyond that—no idea!

Juanita, I can only imagine how the past few days have impacted the feelings of exhaustion and burnout that you were experiencing when you began your time away.

Take your time to sort things out, but believe me, I miss you and the entire office misses you.

We need you back in the fight!

I'll let you know of developments.

Janice

# THIRTEEN

"Tell my useless brother that I'll make it to the ranch before dinner. Since my niece, my wife, and all of my hired help are way too busy to actually spend time working, I have no choice but keep the shop closed for a few more days." Foster gave a despondent look as if he had just been sentenced to solitary confinement.

"Poor Uncle Foster. Such a neglected human soul." Juanita pecked his cheek as she skipped through the shop. The shop is closed so you can keep all doors locked. Your wife is away. You have no customers, or friends I might add. Aunt Flo needs my help preparing dinner and Ernie is desperate for Brad's advice on all kinds of ranching matters." Standing in the doorway, Juanita pointed to Brad sitting in his truck outside the shop. "My carriage and driver have arrived. See you soon in Aunt Flo's kitchen. And whatever happens, do not be late."

With a dismissive wave and a smile of affection, Foster muttered a curt, "Good riddance. And be sure to tell Brad and my brother that they are nothing more than drugstore cowboys and wannabe law officers."

———

Leaving Red River and beginning the climb up Bobcat Pass, Juanita and Brad drove in peaceful silence. After cresting the pass, the giant sprawl of meadows and ranchland, as always, delivered a sense of awe. "This land will always be magical for me." Juanita looked to Brad. "Aren't we lucky to be here?"

"Lucky doesn't begin to describe it. Every time I am here, I think back to the days of my life spent in big cities. That was my life then because I had no choice. But I sure as heck never want to see New York City, Washington, DC, or any of those sprawling messes again." Turning to Juanita with a smile, Brad finished his thought. "I suppose I can tolerate Albuquerque. I'll sacrifice just to humor you."

Throwing her hands up in exasperation, Juanita fired back. "To humor me? To humor me! Please! Are you chewing those magic mushrooms again? I'm the one who is making noises about leaving Albuquerque. It is yours truly who has been trying to have a serious discussion about a lifestyle change. I'm the only one here with any ideas of leaving big city life. Maybe trying something new and different is way beyond you." Juanita crossed her arms defiantly. "If it involves anything beyond your fly rod or enchiladas, you begin to stutter and wet your pants."

"Good grief. I didn't mean to light you on fire. Let's get through tonight's dinner with Flo and Ernie. On the drive home we will talk serious talk about you walking away from prosecuting."

"Actually, I think it's kinda cute when you stutter and wet your pants." Juanita winked. "The stuttering part is definitely cute. Wetting your pants, hmm, not so much."

Just before turning from the highway onto the road leading to Ernie's house, Brad looked to the sky. "We may both be stuttering if those storm clouds in the west continue to build. We better keep our eyes open."

Brad's attention was focused on a threatening sky. He failed to pay attention to the red pickup truck that had been following them in the distance. Even if he had been paying attention, he could not have known of the phone call Boone Curtis placed to Luther Birdwell.

# FOURTEEN

The aroma was beyond heavenly. Flo moved about her kitchen with the grace of an Olympic skater. Every fraction of every inch of the space she claimed for her and her alone had been traversed at least a million times. She could prepare a feast for dozens while blindfolded. Flo needed more than two eyes, however, to keep track of her husband and the rambunctious dog he had just invited to the house.

Seeing the withering look from his wife over the presence of the dog, Ernie became defensive. "Oh, come on, Spud. He'll calm down and be fine in no time. Poor dog just wants to be with the family." Ernie glanced around the room to be sure others were paying attention. "Hell, Flo, he even likes you. He's a good judge of character. He and his big heart forgive you of past sins and your wicked ways."

"The only family that mutt knows is junkyard dogs." Flo corrected herself. "Make that barnyard dogs. The only time he's not looking to make trouble is when he's out with you, stomping around in mud or manure. And he much prefers manure."

Juanita and Brad stood by the kitchen window. Sipping iced tea, they tried not to laugh out loud as Flo and Ernie went at each other. Foster had already taken a seat at the table. His chair, leaning back on two legs, had become a rocker. He made no attempt to hide his amusement over the antics of his brother and sister-in-law.

The dog continued slinking about the kitchen, his nose on high alert. Depending on whether it was Flo or Ernie speaking, he responded to multiple names. If he heard Ernie's voice, he was accustomed to Good Old Boy, My Good Friend, Pal, or sometimes Bud. He had long ago learned to ignore Flo for the insults that almost always accompanied her hurtful names. He just wagged his tail when he heard her frustrated proclamations. "Dumb-Ass Dog" and "Filthy Flea-Ridden Mongrel" were simply terms of endearment. Over time, he had learned to recognize when Flo's frustrations were truly serious. When her shouts became shrill, it was time for evasive maneuvers. Becoming invisible was a skill that he was quite proud of. Shrill signaled danger.

Shrill was happening now. His first warning was the spatula that flew across the kitchen, nearing the speed of light. Missing his head by a whisker, Flo's hysterical threat came through loud and clear. "You filthy, despicable beast, get out of this kitchen before I cut your gonads off and feed them to the cat!"

Reluctantly but quickly removing his deeply embedded nose from the crotch of Juanita's blue jeans, the dog suddenly decided he preferred to be on the porch. Belly dragging the floor and sad, brown eyes alert for incoming fire, he slithered out the door in search of safer territory.

With a second spatula resting in a fully cocked arm, Flo's eyes searched the room for anyone daring to laugh. The only thing that prevented the launching of a second aerial attack was that everyone was laughing. Even Juanita, her face crimson beneath brown skin, could not contain herself.

Recognizing the tactical disadvantage of negative public opinion, Flo used the spatula as a commanding wand. With the authority of a combat-hardened general, she directed her guests to sit exactly where she wished. The table was soon a blur of busy hands and chattering voices. Platters of roast beef, gravy, potatoes, fresh vegetables, and home-baked bread were passed in a frenzy.

# FIFTEEN

Thunder growled in a darkening sky. Gusting winds carried the smell of foreboding.

———

Flo's heart softened. Conditional pardon was granted. Ernie's dog, terrified of storms, was given the privilege of at least one more sunrise.

———

Following Foster's announcement that he intended to spend the night and mooch more food and booze from his brother, hurried farewells were exchanged. "You don't have much time before dark." Ernie looked to the sky. "I don't like the looks of this. You might should think about going home through Angel Fire and Taos Canyon. Bobcat Pass can be ornery in a storm. It's a few miles longer but probably worth it." Ernie's caution came as Brad started his engine and Juanita fastened the seatbelt on the passenger side. With final waves, Brad pulled away, heading toward the highway.

———

"Now, what the hell are they doing going off that direction?" The red pickup truck roared to life as Boone Curtis hit the ignition.

"Probably looking to avoid the pass with a storm coming. Don't matter none to me. One way good as the other for what we're going to do." Luther Birdwell lifted the weapon he had last used to slaughter an owl. With the truck's windows tightly closed, mechanical sounds of a twelve-gauge shotgun echoed ominously within the cab. A cylinder packed with gunpowder and steel pellets now rested in the weapon's chamber.

"Let's go, Boone. Nailing them two fuckers on a stormy-ass night is just perfect." Birdwell cradled the shotgun across his lap.

The red pickup truck pulled out from beneath a canopy of trees and eased onto the highway.

———

"I hope to heck we are doing the right thing by taking this route." Juanita and Brad looked through the truck's windows to evaluate the sky. Brad spoke with a worried tone. "Your Uncle Ernie is right about Bobcat Pass being dangerous in a storm. But Taos Canyon is no picnic either. Keep your fingers crossed that we get through the canyon before the storm hits."

"All fingers crossed. Legs and toes crossing as we speak." Casting another look out of her window, Juanita appeared to be talking to the sky. "I don't know, Brad. This doesn't feel right. At least not for this time of year. I'm thinking this looks like one of those early spring or late winter storms that come sneaking over the mountains. When those bad boys hit, they bring real trouble." Juanita spoke softly. "September is supposed to be a gentle month. A time of changing colors and picking apples." Turning to Brad, Juanita spoke across the cab. "Skies that look this vicious cause me to think that God is angry about something. Maybe he intends to teach us mere mortals a lesson."

———

Lightning fractured the sky. Thunder was seconds behind. As Juanita and Brad drove, winds swept up 13,000-foot Wheeler Peak as if it were an ant hill. Gales then descended into Moreno Valley with fury. When they arrived, Juanita and Brad felt their truck rock on its springs.

———

Ernie walked through his house. "All secure, folks. Spud, get us some candles ready. A bad one is on the way. I suspect we'll be going to bed with no lights."

———

Flo's heart softened. Gentle strokes helped to calm the trembling dog curled in her lap. Storms were more terrifying than even Flo when she became shrill.

———

Raindrops, initially sporadic, struck in big, heavy globs. Intensity grew. Projectiles of water began to pummel the earth as millions of meteorites. Noise within Brad's truck became deafening. Turning on headlights, Brad noticed headlights of another vehicle following in the distance.

———

"Let the bastards get past Angel Fire. Too many people and too much to go wrong. Once they get beyond all them buildings and people, we can pick the time and place." Birdwell ran a loving hand over the shotgun. "Don't let them get too far ahead of us. When it's time, we need to be able to pull up close and do it real fast."

Curtis nodded as he increased their speed. "Damn, it's raining hard."

Like a cat stalking an unsuspecting bird, Boone Curtis and the red pickup truck calculated the pace.

———

"I can't believe that twenty miles back, we were sitting at Aunt Flo's table having a banquet." Juanita's laugh was muffled by the clamor Mother Nature was delivering. "I don't think there has ever been a time that I visited Aunt Flo and Uncle Ernie that I didn't leave their house laughing. Those two are characters made for a movie."

"Yeah, but don't forget the dog. As I recall, he delivered a few laughs of his own this evening. And at your expense I'm happy to say."

Squinting his eyes and looking ahead through the rain, Brad spotted two vehicles sitting at the intersection of the main road leading out of Angel Fire. "Well, at least we aren't the only fools out in this mess. We have company a good way behind us." He gave a nod toward the vehicles waiting to enter the highway. "And it looks like these two folks just ahead of us are crazy enough to join the party."

Clearing a blinking orange light at the Angel Fire intersection, Brad checked his mirrors. The two SUV-style vehicles had waited for Brad to pass in order to safely enter the highway. Focused on adjusting the defrost control for the front window, Juanita was oblivious to other vehicles.

The first SUV made an entry onto the highway and fell into a safe following distance. Brad viewed his mirror in amazement as the second SUV attempted to enter the highway but was cut off by a deliberate acceleration of the vehicle that had for some time been following in the distance.

The abrupt and dangerous maneuver caused Brad to take a second look at the offending vehicle. It was a red pickup truck.

"Weather or no weather, I guess idiots and jerks will always be on the road." Brad muttered his frustration to the clamor of the storm.

———

"Damn it Boone, you got too far behind. Now we have us a carload of Texas tourists between us and them shitbirds. Probably a bunch of Mormons behind us." Lifting a paper cup to his mouth, Luther spit. "Kiss my ass. Now we got no choice but to hope these sightseers and missionaries turn off the road somewhere and leave us alone with Romeo and Juliet." Luther again spit. "Dammit to hell!"

———

Something didn't feel right. Driving through the storm was bad enough. The curving climb after leaving Angel Fire was treacherous under any circumstance. With driving rain and hurricane-like wind gusts, the steering wheel felt inadequate. Brad wished for floor pedals to act as rudders in navigating a highway that was partially submerged. But it was more than wild weather. Why in the world would that red pickup truck have done something so foolish in such terrible conditions? And why was the pickup truck now following dangerously close to the SUV that had entered the highway at Angel Fire?

Red pickup truck.

The knot in Brad's stomach returned. Could it be?

Red pickup truck. A slaughtered deer. Head severed from the body.

Red pickup truck.

Luther Birdwell standing on river's edge. Crossbow aimed.

Brad swallowed. Should he say something to Juanita? Had his fear of the storm kicked his imagination into overdrive?

What should have been the last gasp of dusk was a faded hope. Black clouds shrouded the last glimmers of twilight and wind blew darkness into the valley. Lightning blazed in ghostly moments. Trees bowed like grass.

Muscles in Brad's arms began to ache.

It was the red pickup. He knew it in his gut. It was Luther Birdwell.

With the sound of a cannon blast, thunder exploded directly over their truck. Juanita involuntarily gasped. "Oh my God!"

Brad gripped the wheel even harder.

---

"Come on, Boone. Get around them damn tourists. Get me up close to Romeo the Bambi lover. I'll blast that chili pepper-loving fucker straight to hell. If I can get one good round off, they'll probably fly off the road and won't nobody even find them for a week." Birdwell pulled the shotgun up, snuggling it into his shoulder.

"Hold on, for Christ's sake. I'll get around these crazy shitbirds when I can." Curtis growled his thoughts to Birdwell. "I ain't gonna kill me and you both just cause you're all excited. We got no weight in the ass end of this truck. We're fishtailing like crazy already. If I take a curve too fast, it's me and you that won't be found for a week. Cool your balls, Luther."

---

"Thank heaven for that SUV behind us." Brad intended for the prayer to remain within his head, but the words slipped out in a whisper.

"Everything okay?" Juanita placed a hand on Brad's leg as she spoke.

Heart pounding, Brad remained silent. Frequent glances into mirrors became a rhythm—the road ahead—relentless headlights behind.

Frequent curves in the road offered moments of reprieve when the following vehicles became lost to view. But the reprieve was always short-lived. With the rounding of each curve, the two sets of headlights reappeared almost as one. The red pickup truck was now following the SUV dangerously close.

For the first time in miles, Brad saw a single vehicle approaching from the oncoming direction. Headlights of a high-profile delivery vehicle passed in a blinding spray of water. Wipers hammered furiously. Brad watched as the red taillights of the delivery vehicle faded. He then stared in disbelief at what unfolded within the parameters of his mirrors. The red pickup truck had apparently attempted to pass the SUV on a curve. It came headlight to headlight with the oncoming delivery truck. The SUV careened into the road's flooded shoulder in a dizzying spin. The delivery truck teetered, precariously close to a complete roll-over. An overcorrect. A skid. The delivery vehicle plunged into an embankment off the highway. Brad saw only a blur of lights as the truck rolled onto its side. In stunned horror, Brad watched as the red pickup truck fishtailed wildly, on the brink of disaster. Regaining command of the pavement, the headlights were again straight. Brad realized the vehicle was now accelerating with reckless speed. Propelled by maniacal commands, headlights of the pickup truck streaked toward Juanita and Brad. Within seconds, glaring headlights were upon them, flooding the cab with the light of artificial day only inches behind.

There was no longer any doubt. His imagination was not out of control. It was indeed the red pickup truck. Luther Birdwell was back.

A voice, familiar but faint, reached Brad's distracted ears. It was Juanita. She was seated beside him. Warmth of her hand was on his leg. "Brad, what's wrong? Why is that crazy person riding our bumper? Something is bad wrong."

---

"Good job, Boone. Keep 'em blinded. Get the nose of the truck right up his ass. Hit the horn while you're at it. Scare the living hell out of the little shits. I'm gonna crank a round right through their window."

Releasing his seat belt and lowering the window in a single motion, Birdwell gasped. Wind shrieked as it blasted through the opening. Water blew through the cab like an icy centrifuge.

Extending his body and shotgun through the window, Luther was unprepared for the shock. Rain exploding onto his bandaged face felt like shrapnel. Unable to keep his eyes open, he gasped for air. Blindly pointing the shotgun, Luther closed his eyes and pulled the trigger.

Screaming obscenities at Birdwell to close his window, Boone Curtis felt his mind swirling in surreal vertigo. His own lights had become blinding. Reflecting in rain and from the rear of Brad's truck, his eyes felt scorched. He felt the truck sway. Ears ringing in deafening concussion from the shotgun blast, Curtis could not see. He could not hear. His brain felt like it was melting. A tire left the road. Gravel hammered the undercarriage like machine gun fire. The vehicle entered a skid. Gravity, wind, water, and laws of physics assumed control of the pickup truck.

Luther retreated into the cab with the shotgun. With no seatbelt harness to secure him, his body tossed as if on a carnival ride. Stunned, gasping, and wheezing, Luther fought to comprehend the violent forces assaulting his body.

———

The blaring horn sounded like it came from within his own cab. Dazzling light and ear-shattering noise singed the air. Relying on instinct over reason, Brad steered his truck into the left lane. In the same motion, he reached for Juanita. With a handful of hair and a violent yank, Brad heard his own voice in a scream. "Down!"

Somewhere within frantic moments and within the mirrors of his truck, the muzzle flash of a weapon registered in Brad's brain. Shattering glass. A sickening thud of shotgun pellets penetrating seat cushions. Brad felt a shudder ripple through his vehicle. The rear section of the truck roared as wind, water, and shards of glass became passengers.

The headlights receded. The horn no longer blared. The storm roared through a demolished back window.

Brad drove. At least for the moment, he had no headlights in his mirrors. "Juanita, are you okay?" Everything had happened in an instant. He had no sense of time. "Juanita, are you okay?" Brad heard his own voice scream.

Darkness obscured the daze in Juanita's eyes as she lifted her body back into her seat. "What in the name of God is going on?" The roar of the storm coming from the rear of the vehicle slowly registered. Juanita looked to Brad. She turned her head to view what she was hearing. Wind, water, and carnage.

"It's Luther Birdwell, Juanita. It's Luther Birdwell. I'm sure Boone Curtis is with him."

Desperate to tell Juanita what had happened, Brad was equally desperate to focus on the road ahead but aware of danger that lurked from behind. Searching his mirrors, he did not see headlights. How long would the reprieve last? Shoulders hunched and heart thundering, Brad drove.

Trying to process what was happening, Brad's mind raced. Forcing his brain to function, he replayed the images he had seen in his mirrors. It was a blur. Another replay. Things became more clear. The pickup truck had careened, out of control. But what had happened after that? Brad had no idea if his pursuer had flipped, crashed, or recovered. Seconds passed. If Birdwell and Curtis had not crashed, if they had survived, they would come again. Of that, he was certain. Brad continued to think. The men knew they were wanted. They were evil. They were desperate. Above all, they were crazy.

Headlights appeared in the mirror. Birdwell and Curtis had survived. They were coming again.

———

"There they are!" Still adrenaline-fueled, Birdwell shouted at the top his lungs. "We gotta catch them bastards fast. If they make it to Taos, too many people. We ain't got a chance if they make it to town. Hit it, Boone. God dammit, hit it!" Mechanisms of a racking shotgun again echoed within the pickup truck.

———

"Juanita, we are in big trouble. Those two idiots are coming again. I've got their lights in my mirror. They're coming fast."

A quick glance over her shoulder to view the oncoming vehicle and the events of the past few seconds began to make sense within Juanita's mind. No longer dazed, she grasped that survival was in the balance. Options sped through her mind. None seemed good. "Can we outrun them?" Her question sounded between despair and desperation.

"Maybe. In this weather, driving crazy is a crap shoot. One of us is going to be the first to crash and burn. If we are the first, they will be on us in a second and we are good as dead." Pressing the accelerator as hard as he dared, Brad tried to remember the remaining few miles into Taos. "If we can catch a curve just right, they will lose sight of us. If there is a side road available, we can try leaving the highway and maybe they won't see us. It's risky as hell and I can't even think of any places to exit."

Lightning fired, igniting the sky. Eerie green illuminated the cab.

Turning for another look, Juanita saw the headlights. She was amazed at the speed with which they were gaining. Her voice was urgent but remained calm. "They're coming fast. But you are right. They have the same problem we have. Going too fast will be deadly." Juanita's brain processed what Brad had said about getting off the highway. "If we can lose them on a curve, how much time would we have without them having us in their sight?"

"A few seconds at best. But where to get off? We can't just pull over. We have to find enough cover that they won't be able to see us."

With the sounds of an artillery attack, sheets of water continued the assault on Brad's truck.

"I know exactly where we can make our turn. If we can just make it before they get too close. And if a curve in the road will only help us out." Juanita stared through the front window. Her brain calculating.

Taking his eyes away from the road and mirrors for a blink, Brad looked at Juanita. "Holy Jesus, Juanita. Talk to me! Where the hell are you talking about?"

"I'm pretty sure that we just passed the sign for Shady Brook. The road to the cabin will be on the left any second now." Juanita turned to Brad. "It's where we went with Ed Romero. If they don't see us make the turn, it might work."

In flashing moments of silent deliberation, Juanita and Brad were no longer aware of the storm. They no longer heard the roar that came from the destroyed rear window. Every thought was of escape and survival.

"Good idea and I sure don't have a better one. Let's do it. I'm watching the mirror for lights. You look for the turn." Brad slowed the truck. It would be a sudden turn and their current speed was way too fast. There was no other choice.

"I'm watching."

"We have headlights. They can see us for sure. They're coming hard."

"No turn yet."

"We have a curve, Juanita. They can't see us. Please, God, please!"

"Turn! Now!" Shouting her command, Juanita grabbed onto the dashboard in anticipation of the jolting she knew was to come.

Brake. Tires on water, slipping. Skid. Tires in mud. Truck convulsing. Sickness in stomach. Seatbelts. Centrifugal force. Listing. Teetering.

The truck righted. Tires clawed into mud. In a final half-spin, the truck lurched to a halt. Positioned sideways in the road, the rear tires hung precariously over a steep ditch. They had made it.

Lights off. Kill engine. Pray.

Turning in their seats, Juanita and Brad peered through darkness. Eyes fixated on the highway. They forgot to breathe. Lungs burned.

Columns of light pierced the rain on the highway above. The truck passed. Darkness again.

Collapsing into his seat, Brad closed his eyes as he exhaled. "They didn't see us."

Juanita shivered. "I'm freezing, Brad. I thought we were going to die."

Speaking into darkness, Brad voiced thoughts as they ran through his mind. "We're not clear yet, Juanita. It won't take them long to figure out what happened. I don't see them just giving up and driving away. I think they will turn around and come looking for a place we could have escaped. It's going to be easy to find. We can't just sit here and wait."

"What about getting back on the highway and going in the opposite direction?"

"That's exactly what I would like to do but I don't think we can pull it off. The truck is pointed downhill. With four-wheel drive, I think I can move forward and head to the meadow. If I try a three-point turn to get us headed back up hill, we are going to be stuck. I remember this road well. It's barely a trail, not a road at all. It's solid trees and deep ditches on both sides. Until we reach the meadow, there is no way in hell we would have a place to turn around. To get back on the highway, we would have to go all the way down to the meadow, make a turn, and then climb back up." Brad shook his head. "I'm afraid we might very well meet them head on. They have a shotgun, Juanita. I know damned well that's what they used to blow out our window."

Frantic for answers, neither of them spoke.

Juanita's voice quivered. "Maybe we should run? Make them chase us."

"You're wearing flip-flops, Juanita. In ten feet, you would be barefooted."

Silence became deafening within the vacuum of options.

———

"Where the hell are they?" Luther Birdwell and Boone Curtis leaned forward, straining to see. Squinting eyes peered beneath furrowed brows. They saw nothing. Their senses and logic quickly told them that they had been tricked.

"We was gaining fast on 'em. No way in hell did they gain a bunch of distance on us." Pumping brakes and spewing obscenities, Curtis brought the pickup truck to a halt. Twisting the wheel, putting the vehicle into a spinning blur of rubber and water, he jammed the gas pedal to the floor. "Them shits got off the highway."

"Fuck! Fuck! Fuck!" Slamming a fist onto the dash, Birdwell screamed. "Don't go too fast, Boone. We gotta be able to see where they turned."

———

"I'm willing to try something, Brad. It's all I can think of."

"I sure as hell have no ideas. If you can think of something, let's hear it. It's got to happen fast."

Her throat choking in panic, Juanita managed to continue. "If we go to the meadow, can we drive across it without getting stuck?"

"Yes, think so."

"Go to the arroyo. Go to where the murders happened. That was the only crossing. Can we make it?"

"Holy Jesus. I don't know."

"Remember what Ed Romero told us about that very spot? Where the creek makes such a sharp turn. He said floods cause debris to collect there."

Their eyes locked within darkness. Juanita spoke as her mind raced. "Remember that pile of tree trunks? They were cut smooth, no branches. Stacked several feet high. The trees are long but not very big around."

"God almighty. I think you're onto something." Brad hit the ignition. Lights on, in gear with four wheels engaged, he steered the truck down the twisting trail. Lurching over rocks and newly washed ditches, the truck practically flew in short bursts. Despite seatbelts, their heads banged against walls of the truck's cabin, their bodies jolted about like dolls. There were terrifying moments when all four tires were in the air simultaneously. Bone-jarring thuds when they again met ground.

Springs, shocks, and tires. With a silent prayer for survival, Brad pressed even harder.

Pitching dangerously, Brad forced the vehicle through the final twist in the trail. Like a welcoming oasis, open meadow unfolded before them. Legs aching, he pressed the accelerator. Shoulders and arms felt like springs, Brad again forced the truck. Meadow grasses flew underneath the truck in a misty haze. Accelerating, speed increasing, mud hammered the undercarriage.

Setting his course from memory, Brad raced along what he hoped to be the path leading from the cabin to the creek. His headlights caught the far bank of the arroyo. Palms slick with sweat, he gripped even harder.

Reaching the gentle decline that led to the creek, Brad lifted his foot from the pedal. Saturated soil collapsed like a sponge beneath the weight of the truck. Mud, congealing onto tires, acted as a brake, quickly slowing the truck's momentum. Juanita gripped the dashboard, straining to see what lay ahead. Dread and disbelief turned their stomachs. Headlights, falling on what they recalled as a trickling creek, now illuminated a seething monster. Roiling water, brown with mud, tore through the arroyo. Foamy froth reflected in headlights like spit from an angry dragon.

"Holy shit!"

"Oh my God!"

Their voices rising to heaven in unison, Brad stomped the accelerator.

They were in water. Were the tires touching bottom? Brad wasn't sure. He felt the truck drift, beginning to float. The rear end surrendered to the current, swinging downstream. Point of no return. Spinning wheels. Front tires touched land. With the groan of a beast fighting for life, the truck's engine gave an exhausted heave. With four tires again gripping land, the truck launched. Catapulting up the river's bank, throwing Juanita and Brad back into their seats.

"Holy Jesus!" Releasing the accelerator, Brad wrenched the wheel, forcing the truck into an upslope and sideways skid. Sinking into mud, the halt was almost instantaneous. Correcting his steering to the desired direction, Brad accelerated again. Full power. The truck lunged, covering the final few feet to their destination. Brakes slammed. Another halt.

Killing engine and lights, Juanita and Brad allowed their bodies to collapse into their seats. Sucking air in frantic gasps, wheezing lungs were in concert with the noise coming from the shattered rear window. Concealed behind the pile of stacked tree trunks, the back end of Brad's truck touched the pyramid of logs. Could they be seen?

Darkness was absolute.

"I have to get out, Juanita. I have to be able to see. No other way to know if they are still with us."

"I'm coming with you."

Their eyes met, exchanging urgency in absolute blackness. "Move fast, Juanita. The cab light could give us away."

Juanita's nod of understanding was felt rather than seen.

"Okay. On three. One. Two. Three."

Doors opened and closed in a heartbeat. Icy rain stole their breath. Moments were needed to orient their bodies and minds to the feel of a drowning atmosphere. With the sting of a whip, rain tore at their skin.

Instinctively clasping hands, Juanita and Brad inched through the black night. Sliding their feet along the ground rather than stepping, they crept to the end of the stacked timber. Easing their heads around what was their only hope for concealment, they looked back across the meadow. Black void. Nothing.

Lightning arced over their heads. It was so close they could hear the sizzle of an electrified sky. For an instant, the meadow became a still-life work of art. Blue-green in color, trees, grass, rocks, and the cabin shimmered. In a haunting way, it was beautiful.

Darkness again. Nothing but rain.

Thunder exploded. Blunt force of an angry atmosphere hammered.

The lights of the truck simply materialized. With the sinking realization that they were still hunted, dread burrowed into their core. Mesmerized, Juanita and Brad watched as their nightmare continued. The creep of headlights was relentless. Moving through trees and brush, they appeared to slowly sink. Like underwater torches, the lights descended. Unblinking eyes searching for prey.

Juanita and Brad knew. There could be no doubt. Luther Birdwell and Boone Curtis were not giving up.

"The guy is either butt-ass crazy or he's got balls of stone. Gotta be one or the other to come down this piece of shit road on a night like this." Curtis hunched over the wheel, clearly uncomfortable in the situation they had entered.

A harsh laugh and a spit directly onto the pickup's floor came from Birdwell. "Well, Boone, I've long been aware that you ain't very smart. But by God, I honestly do think you might drive this road through a blizzard on Christmas morning if someone was after you with this here shotgun." Another laugh and another spit. "Just keep on doing what you're doing. Before you can say kiss my sweet ass, we'll have both of them where we want 'em. I plan to blow them both halfway to El Paso. Once that's done, we can roll into Taos nice and easy. After we drink us some good whiskey and find a good long fuck, it's Utah for us. That ranger with a snatch between her legs is next. Crazy bitch is probably a Mormon on top of being a damned woman." Birdwell chuckled. "Then, let the manhunt begin. Me and you are gonna be famous, Boone. Famous as movie stars."

A moment of silence followed Birdwell's proclamation. The men searched the meadow in their headlights until Birdwell pointed. "Right there they go. Their tracks are plain as day. Hell fire, Boone, I wish all our tracking jobs was this easy."

Muttering curses, Curtis steered the pickup truck over the meadow. "I can't see a damned thing except for their tracks." Squinting over the wheel, he spoke again. "I know this country well enough to say there's gotta be a hill or a mountain ahead of us. This flat-ass meadow can't go on forever. I'm gonna stop and light things up. We need to scope what the hell we are getting into. I ain't liking this, Luther." Curtis continued to spew obscenities as he slowed the vehicle. "What the hell we got this big-ass light for anyway if it ain't for something like this?"

"By God, Boone, you just might be right for once in your life. There damned sure is a hill up ahead of us. Their tracks is heading straight to it. They're up there hiding. I can feel it. They're hiding like little scared kittens. Move on up just a bit more. Get a little closer to the hill and we'll light 'em up like Main Street on Christmas Eve."

Creeping over Brad's tire tracks in the grass, Curtis shook his head as his voice became more skeptical. "I don't like this, Luther. Don't like it at all."

"You just drive. I'll do the liking. Move on up another thirty feet or so."

Stopping the pickup truck, Curtis flicked a switch. A spotlight mounted outside the driver's door fired its massive beam. Filament and electricity, a basic tool of poachers, blasted unimaginable candle power onto the hillside. Rotating the handle inside his cab, Curtis directed a beam of light across rocks, boulders, and trees of the facing hillside.

"You got it, Boone. Right there. That big pile of tree trunks. Swing it back a tad." Glee was in Birdwell's voice as Curtis adjusted the light. "I can see their tracks leading right up to that stack of trees. They're playing house up there behind the woodpile. Now ain't that just the sweetest thing."

Without speaking, Curtis again moved the beam. Slowly twisting the handle within his palm, he directed light away from the stacked trees. Tracing the route of freshly disturbed soil, what had happened in Juanita and Brad's race for survival was a story easily read. "Yep, that's where they are. That hillside is too damned rough and steep for 'em to go anywhere else in this damned flood."

Curtis turned to look across the cab to Birdwell. Doubt brimmed in his eyes. "Think maybe you got your scared kittens, Luther. You happy? Maybe we should think about leaving them here. Leave 'em scared shitless. Head to Utah and do what you want to do there. We have to live through tonight before we can even think about taking our asses to Utah."

Ignoring Birdwell's profanity-laced response, Curtis continued moving the light beam farther down the hill. He stopped. "Mother of God, Luther. Look at that water. Son of a bitch. We sure as hell don't need to be fucking around with that."

"What the hell you saying, Boone?"

Speaking slowly, Curtis leveled his eyes to meet Birdwell's face.

"It ain't too late to turn this truck around and high tail our asses out of here. Maybe we should forget about this. We've scared 'em halfway to hell. Think maybe that's good enough? Give a good look at that damned river, Luther. Think about this. You want to be famous, or you want to be drowned and dead?"

Studying the water, Birdwell groped about in vain for his cup. Unable to find it, he again spit onto the floor. For a moment, the cab was silent. "The two love birds just crossed, didn't they? They're up there right now, Boone. They are up there hiding and shaking." Birdwell turned to Curtis, his eyes glaring in the dim light. "Their last prayer is for us to turn chicken-liver and drive away." Shaking his head and pointing across the water to the stacked trees, Birdwell's voice became a sadistic growl. "Ain't gonna happen, Boone. Not as long as I'm breathing. I let 'em go once. Not going to happen again. If them two can cross that little pissant stream, we can sure as hell cross that little pissant stream. Turn that damned spotlight off, grab a hold of your pecker and let's go."

Flicking the spotlight off, hands gripping the wheel with eyes closed, Boone Curtis gripped the wheel and lowered his head. It was decision time.

The pickup truck shook as Curtis revved the engine. Its scream became a part of the storm's fury. Uncertain if the maneuver was to build power for the water crossing or to fortify his own courage, Curtis stomped on the accelerator. Decision made. Gear stick yanked. Gears slammed. Truck catapulted.

———

The river waited.

———

"They're coming, Juanita. Stay clear."

Moving through darkness, Brad sprinted to the driver's door. Engine on, forward. Only a few feet. Reverse. Hit the gas pedal hard.

Bam! The truck rammed into the stacked trees. Wheels spinning, mud flying into the night, Brad repeated the maneuver. Forward. Reverse. Forward. Reverse. The truck shuddered. Metal crumpled like cardboard. Again. Harder.

Angry groans crept from deep within the layered timbers. The first tree shifted. Another battering jolt from the truck. Bouncing upon saturated ground, the log finally rolled. Gravity pulled. The tree tumbled. Plunging into the torrent, it hesitated for a split second, then streaked like a missile.

---

A second tree fell. A third. An avalanche.

---

Plunging into a riverbed of shifting mud, wheels began to spin without traction. The truck settled. Water rose over sideboards. Sensing disaster, Curtis frantically shifted gears. He searched for traction. None came. The pickup truck began to sink.

RPMs screamed from within a tortured engine. The pickup truck rocked. The rear end was the first to drift.

Sucking a hard breath of panic, he turned his head and eyes upstream. Through darkness, Boone Curtis saw the doorway of eternity.

---

Desperate to see through rain and night, Juanita and Brad stood frozen in the moment. In a dazzling display of cosmic power, lightning fractured the sky. Macabre light from fiery fingers flashed over the meadow and river. Lasting only for a second, the image was stark. A bearded man, comprehending his final seconds of life, was the only thing Juanita and Brad saw. In the blackness that followed, the cacophony of thunder, shattering glass, and collapsing metal became a single, howling shriek.

# SIXTEEN

Shivering, Juanita and Brad sat in silence. The heater, blasting at full strength, struggled against the chill that openly flowed through the gaping hole that had once been the rear window of Brad's truck. For the moment, they were content to sit in silence, each processing the blur of what they had just experienced: The highway, the storm, a blaring horn, and blinding lights. The blast of a shotgun. A twisting road, a flooded meadow. A torrential river. Tree trunks that had become angels of salvation. Angels of death.

Minutes passed. Shivering slowly subsided. Hearts slowed and breathing calmed. They no longer shivered. More time passed. The rain slowed.

His voice sounding strange to his own ears, Brad finally spoke. "Juanita, you need to call Janice Weathers. Tell her what has happened. It will be much better for her or one of the investigators to call the Taos Police Department. If the call is from someone official, it will help cut through the craziness of all this. I'm not even sure who will have jurisdiction. We're going to let someone else worry about that."

A slow up-and-down movement of her head accompanied Juanita's reply. Staring out the window, she responded in a soft voice. "I agree. I've been thinking about just that. Searching for the right words to explain what happened. Thank God I'll be talking to a friend who knows the history of all this. You know, Brad, my life's work is presenting evidence to a jury. It's my job to lay out facts in a way that enables everyday people to understand what it means to be the victim of a crime. It's my job to bring together the right words, to tell a story, that brings to life the horror so many victims endure."

Turning to face Brad, Juanita's voice had a distant tone. "I've always empathized with the victims who came to me." Juanita moved her head and sadness entered her voice. Struggling to put into words the thoughts that jumbled within her mind, Juanita continued. "Tonight has given me a whole new perspective of what it means to be a victim. I don't know how in the world I could ever convey to a jury the fear that I experienced this evening. Police and prosecutors, they have an obligation to never lose sight of what victims endure. But we are lucky. We handle a case and then move on." Juanita's voice was heavy. "But for victims, oh my Lord, so many times it is never over for them."

Reaching across the cab for Juanita's hand, Brad paused before speaking. "I understand, Juanita. But let me tell you something. I know you. I know your heart. You have never forgotten a victim that came to you. Maybe that's why you've been struggling. The weight of so many damaged souls can become terribly heavy."

"Maybe so, Brad. Thank you for saying those words. But until a person is actually victimized, I'm not sure an outsider can ever really understand what many innocent people are so often forced to endure. Tonight's nightmare has been a lesson for me. I have been a victim." Juanita paused. "It's going to take some time and soul searching for me to get my head straight."

"Take all the time you need. Days, weeks, or months, I don't care. I'm going to be with you every step." The cab was again quiet except for the roaring of the heater. Juanita stared out her window and gave a nod.

"Just for tonight, give it some time. Let your emotions settle before making a call to Janice. There is no rush because it's going to take a good long time for anyone to get here anyway. We sure as hell aren't going anywhere, no matter who responds. Even after the river goes down, we will probably need a winch to get us out. It's my guess that the logjam we created is going to be there for quite a while."

Juanita simply nodded but said nothing as she leaned back into her seat, closing her eyes.

Brad left her to her thoughts.

After another extended period of silence, Juanita opened her eyes and glanced out the window. Seemingly startled by what she saw, she reached across the cab, touching Brad's hand. "Look, Brad, the rain has stopped. We haven't seen lightning or heard thunder for some time now. I think the storm has ended."

"Yeah, things are settling. Clouds are breaking up. I'm pretty sure we will be seeing stars for the rest of the night. In fact, I'm going to turn the truck around, so we are facing the meadow. That will give us a much better view of the sky as we go through the night. I sure don't see us sleeping."

Once Brad had turned his truck to face the meadow, everything seemed more peaceful. Following the mayhem of the storm, sounds of the truck's heater and the water from the flooding creek had become scarcely noticeable. As the sky calmed, so did emotions. Brad turned the heating fan off. Minutes passed. Hearts and minds made peace. The river settled.

---

Brad could sense something stirring in Juanita. He waited. It was her time.

"I've made a decision, Brad." Turning her head toward Brad, Juanita spoke through the night. "I need you to be with me. You may not agree, but there is something I have to do before I call Janice. I'm asking you to be with me."

Returning Juanita's gaze in the starlight, Brad responded quietly. "I think I know what you are going to say, but go ahead. Tell me."

"Before I can possibly talk with Janice, before I can even begin to describe what happened tonight, I have to go down there. I have to go to the creek, to where everything ended. I can't imagine what we are going to find or what we are going to see." Juanita sighed deeply. "But there is no way I can process what happened to us tonight until I see for myself." Juanita's eyes searched Brad's face for a reaction.

Tapping his fingers on the wheel, Brad looked up into the sky. Releasing a sigh of his own, he again looked at Juanita. "I knew this was coming. I suspect it's the prosecutor thing. You have to see it all. Feel, touch, and smell every little detail. That's the only way you can tell the story to a jury. I understand, sweetheart. And, of course, I'll go with you."

Both were quiet. The creek that had been roaring was slowly calming. It was the only sound in the night.

"Okay, let's go. There is a flashlight in the glove box." Stepping out of the truck and closing the door behind him, Brad waited. Juanita's hand was soon within his.

Juanita directed the light beam as they cautiously moved through wet grass, the muddy soil slippery beneath their feet. Even though the creek was noticeably calmer, as they neared its edge, surging strength remained ominous. Keeping the beam focused on the ground before them, the water remained in darkness and out of view. The thumping sound of tree trunks, colliding and grinding, told Juanita and Brad exactly where they were. They stopped walking and stood still. They listened. They thought.

Only feet away from the creek, the sounds coming from the water combined with the knowledge of what they were about to see created a feeling that they stood in another world. Muddy water swirling, logs in perpetual collision, human beings entombed. A graveyard of water.

An audience of billions of stars waited. It was Juanita's decision of when to cast the beam of her light.

The scene was surreal. Logs, thirty feet in length, bobbed like corks in brown water. Tons of wood collided in a pulverized mass of foam. The debris seemed to snarl in angry mockery of the paltry beam coming from Juanita's flashlight. Appearing as a mere bathtub toy, only the upper half of the cab of the red pickup truck remained above water.

Forcing her arm to move, Juanita adjusted the light. The driver of the pickup truck had apparently taken a direct hit from the butt end of a tree. What was left of the man's head remained attached to his body by strands of tissue. The remaining gory glob sloshed about within the cab. Rising and falling within the water's flow, what had been a human being was mere flotsam. Holding the beam in place, Juanita stared at the ghastly site.

Taking a few steps farther and shifting her light, the body Juanita clearly recognized as Luther Birdwell came into view. Half of Luther extended out from the truck's window where he had apparently tried to escape. His upper torso had been crushed between cascading logs that now held him within their death trap. Luther's eyes remained fully open, staring directly into the beam of Juanita's light. A small crawdad had already discovered the treasure. Startled by the light, the creature halted the beginnings of its feast upon the exposed eyes.

Juanita spoke over her shoulder as she swept her light over the carnage. "Brad, do you realize this is exactly where Ed Romero brought us? This is the very spot where Juanita and Manuel Lujan were murdered. This is where I knelt to touch the water." Juanita inhaled sharply. "When I did that, when I touched that water, I did so with reverence."

Juanita was quiet as she continued to survey the contaminated stains that now fouled a place of sanctity. Brad remained behind her, not speaking. The night belonged to Juanita.

Turning off the light, Juanita stood in silence. Stars shimmered. Seconds passed. Brad did not move. When Juanita spoke, she did so softly and directly to the river. But starlight interceded, carrying her words to the doors of heaven. "Burn in hell, you bastards."

Juanita turned to Brad's embrace.

———

"Janice said that the entire crew is coming. She is driving up early tomorrow morning with the investigator from the Department of Fish and Wildlife and the FBI guy. They all will be at the Taos Police Department at 11:00."

"Thanks for making the call," Brad said. "I suppose no sleep for lots of folks tonight. I doubt there is any way to avoid the gathering turning into a royal cluster. But that's life. When stuff like this happens, we just have to go with the flow."

"You are correct. We'll just do what we have to do."

"While you were on the phone with Janice, I called Ed Romero. He knows everyone in Taos. I'm pretty sure we will see him out here tomorrow morning for all the excitement. There is no way that Ed is going to miss this adventure."

"I hope he shows up." Juanita laughed. "There will be a bunch of serious-faced folks out here. Ed will be a friendly and welcome relief."

Settling in for what was left of the night, Juanita and Brad became warm within their blanket of silence. As if heaven itself directed a celestial performance, night became the stage for a performance of magnificence. Stars, some blue, others green, dangled like icy glitter, frosting the New Mexico sky. The Milky Way shimmered in a veil of horizon-to-horizon brilliance.

"How can there be such beauty looking down on so much evil?" Juanita's question was an observation and did not require an answer. Lost in thoughts of all that had happened since leaving Flo and Ernie's table, they wondered within their own minds. "Isn't it amazing." Juanita again spoke. "After living through a terror that I've never before experienced, I am now safe with you and witnessing beauty that defies description. My soul is at peace. My heart is calm. Just look at this sky. Just look at this marvelous sky." Taking a breath, Juanita invited silence as she pondered. Her thoughts became a whisper. "I feel like I am in a cathedral."

Somewhere between meditation and contemplation, Juanita and Brad passed the night. Earth and sky rotating through the swirl of galaxies. Stars drifting on the black currents of space. The passing of time.

Fingernails dug into Brad's thigh. A gasp from Juanita.

"Oh my God!" Juanita's voice was a hoarse whisper. "Oh my God!

"Juanita, what's wrong?"

"Brad, look in the meadow. Oh my God! Look at the cabin."

His eyes following Juanita's pointing hand, Brad swallowed.

Beneath the dome of the universe, within the tiny cabin, the light of a lantern flickered.

Seconds passed.

Juanita's lips scarcely moved. "A candle in a cathedral."

## SEVENTEEN

With the first hint of dawn, vehicle lights began to appear. As a pink glow became the light of day, people and official-looking equipment moved about like ants. Juanita and Brad walked to the creek's edge. A uniformed officer, accompanied by Ed Romero, greeted them from the opposite side. "Mornin! We've got you a tow truck with a chain and winch on the way." The officer waved. "Looks to me like somebody made quite a mess around here." Shaking his head with a smile, he continued. "You have to be exhausted. As soon as all this is photographed, we'll get you across the River Jordan here so you can be on your way. I'm guessing you might want to get into town for a stack of pancakes and a little rest." The officer laughed. "Between Albuquerque lawyers, game wardens, and FBI folks, nobody in Taos got any sleep at all last night." He paused. "From what I hear, you had a pretty wild night yourselves."

"Yeah, you might say that." Brad spoke as Juanita nodded her head.

With a sly grin, the officer continued. "Ed here asked me to give your truck a thorough search. He thinks you swiped some art from his studio. I told him to relax cause according to most people I know in Taos, his art isn't worth stealing."

Ed Romero's manicured mustache and white teeth glistened in the sunlight. Looking to Juanita and Brad, Ed placed his right hand over his heart. Patting his chest, Ed's words drifted over the creek. "I'll be seeing you in my studio for another cup of tea. I want to hear the things that I'm sure you will never tell the police." His hand again patted his heart.

# EIGHTEEN

After checking in to a longtime favorite bed and breakfast on Kit Carson Road, Juanita and Brad soaked beneath a blessedly hot shower. With no time for a trip to Red River before the 11:00 gathering of investigators, Foster saved the day by delivering a change of clothing. His cheerful demeanor was a weak disguise for the turmoil he felt after hearing only sketchy details of what his niece and Brad had experienced. "A breakfast of huevos rancheros is what your wise old uncle recommends. Stand by, I'm taking you to the best Taos has to offer. Come with me. Do what I say, and all will be well."

Mountains of freshly baked pastries and the aroma of coffee, green chili, and tortillas provided sensory overload. The bustle of life within the landmark café of Taos struck Juanita and Brad as something from a fairy tale. Eyes meeting from across their table, they silently relived their hours of horrors and miracles. Foster sipped coffee without questions or comments. A wise man, he left Juanita and Brad to their private thoughts.

———

The parking area for the Taos Police Department was filled to near capacity. Squeezing between a dilapidated pickup and a state patrol cruiser, Foster killed the engine and grinned. "Okay, I want you to know something. You can have this sorry excuse of a car for as long as you need it. Since what's left of your damned near demolished truck has been impounded by the friendly Taos Police Department, this is my gift to you." With a chuckle he continued. "Now listen to me. Please don't get a wild hair up your rear ends and go off on another adventure. I don't care all that much about you, but I can't afford to have you destroy this poor baby like you destroyed your truck." Foster patted the dashboard. "She's served me for over two hundred thousand miles. I sure would like to keep her in one piece and purring like a happy little kitten."

Pecking her uncle on the cheek, Juanita slid out of the vehicle. "I'm not the one you have to worry about, Uncle Foster." With an accusatory point of a finger toward Brad, she continued. "It's all him. He refuses to grow up. I think he is going to play cops and robbers till he's in a nursing home gumming oatmeal and Jell-O." Juanita hesitated and gave her eyes a sarcastic roll. "Which may very well happen far sooner than he thinks."

———

The conference room of the Taos Police Department was a buzz of activity. Upon entering, Juanita and Brad were met by a blur of strange but friendly faces. The New Mexico State Police, Taos County officials, Taos police officers, the Taos County coroner, and others whose identities remained a mystery shook their hands and offered words of congratulations or comfort.

Spotting the familiar face of Janice Weathers, Juanita and Brad maneuvered through the crowd to be near her. Juanita and Janice embraced in silence. Glenn Snyder from the FBI and Charles Carson from New Mexico Department of Game and Fish grasped Brad's hand, and each gave a hug to Juanita.

A microphone-powered voice commanded attention of the room and the den of dozens of voices became quiet. A lean, square-jawed man in a police uniform spoke. Identifying himself as the chief of police for Taos, he thanked all for showing up on short notice. "Since both subjects of this investigation were federal fugitives, I'm going to turn this meeting over to Janice Weathers of the United States Attorney's office in Albuquerque. Ms. Weathers will organize how statements will be recorded and coordinate the many pieces of evidence that we are dealing with. A great deal of work remains to properly conclude what came very close to tragedy." The chief of police swept his eyes over the room of gathered people. He spoke solemnly. "A very near tragedy for some of our own."

Janice Weathers shuffled her way through the crowd. Reaching the front of the room, she took the microphone and began to speak. Brad felt a nudge in his ribs. Turning, he looked into the face of Glenn Snyder, the young FBI agent he had previously met in Santa Fe.

His expression dead serious, the agent whispered into Brad's ear. "Please, for God's sake, don't tell us that it was a frigging owl that saved your sorry ass this time."

# NINETEEN

Exhaustion invaded every joint and muscle. The culmination of their night with Luther Birdwell and Boone Curtis, followed by hours of interviews and legal documentation, had taken a toll. Juanita and Brad lay in their Red River bedroom, showered and thankful to be alone. With lights off and curtains of the opened window stirring in a breeze, they finally felt able to enjoy the luxury of simply relaxing. Shoulders touching and hands intertwined, they stared at the ceiling and savored quiet. The mere presence of each other was all they wanted.

"I'm exhausted, Brad, but I don't think I can sleep. I still have too many things running through my mind."

Nodding his head in the darkness, Brad placed pressure on Juanita's hand. "I understand. I feel the same way. It's going to take a while for our memories to settle down. Nighttime will probably be the worst."

"If it's okay with you, and you aren't falling asleep, I need to talk."

"Of course. I'm wide awake."

Juanita remained quiet for a moment. "Let's go outside. We can sit on the steps and see the sky. Besides, I think better when I'm sitting. And heaven knows, I'm needing to think."

"Absolutely." Brad rose from the bed. "I'll grab a blanket and meet you on the steps."

Once settled, Juanita and Brad let minutes pass as they huddled together. Just as had happened the previous night, while trapped in Brad's truck, a display of cosmic splendor blazed.

"What a difference. Same sky. Different night." Juanita looked to Brad's face. "But what a different feel. Thank God we are not shivering in that meadow tonight."

"I think we can describe all that happened as the night of mayhem and miracles."

"Good words there, Mr. Poetic." Juanita's elbow gave a jab into Brad's side. "But the way I see it, mayhem and miracles started long before last night. I've lost track of time. But in the name of heaven, just think about the past few days. All that happened is absolutely mind-boggling. A crazy owl and your premonitions started everything. And what a journey we've had since then."

Nothing more was said. Images formed, words echoed. Minds drifted into the galaxy.

Juanita wanted to talk, but she remained hesitant. Brad didn't push. A satellite traversed the sky in a silent glide through the heavens.

"Do you suppose that satellite could see all that happened last night?" Juanita pulled the blanket tighter. "What do you think satellites and stars talk about when people like Luther Birdwell do what they do?"

"I don't know, Juanita." Brad spoke slowly. "After your visitor in the shop, after the cemetery and our trip with Ed Romero, I have no idea what to believe about anything."

"And the light in the cabin?" Juanita looked to Brad. "You saw that just like I did. Don't tell me that somebody up there isn't talking."

Brad did not reply, but Juanita saw his head move up and down.

Again, looking up into the sky, Juanita began to speak. As if the stars were the friends with whom she wished to confide, she directed her words into the void. "I may never fully understand all that has happened during our so-called vacation here in Uncle Foster's shop. But understand or not, I have resolved a few things in my mind."

Brad felt a sigh leave Juanita's body.

"When we arrived here, I was struggling. I wasn't sure if I wanted to continue my life as a lawyer. Prosecuting case after case, felony after felony, with victim after victim. I felt I was on an endless, spinning carousel that never stopped or led anywhere."

"I know you have been struggling." Brad gave her hand a squeeze. "I don't blame you for your feelings."

"Well, my struggles are over. It's absolutely crazy. My mind is so filled with confusing mysteries and unanswered questions that I should be going nuts. But that's not happening. For the first time in months, I am actually seeing things with clarity. This past week or so, and all that it delivered, the good and the bad, I now realize has been a gift."

Continuing to hold Juanita's hand, Brad waited. This was not a time to rush.

Still looking up, her eyes in the heavens and her voice soft, Juanita continued. "If I've lived before in another time or if living today is nothing but a dream, I simply cannot grasp. I don't know for sure what is real. When I wake up tomorrow, will I be in a modern world, a lawyer in a fancy courtroom? Or will I be in a primitive cabin, changing children's hair color?"

Joining Juanita in gazing to the stars, Brad listened but said nothing.

Gathering her thoughts, Juanita took more time. "But whatever world I'm supposed to be living in, one thing has become clear to me. I'm certain of something. God or some sort of power out there," she swept an arm across the sky, "has a purpose for me. I know beyond doubt that every time I send a murderer or rapist to prison, I have dyed the hair of a child and saved a life. It's all the same. Whichever world, it's all the same."

Leaning her head onto Brad's shoulder, Juanita did not speak for moments. "Last night taught me what it means to be a victim. It was horrible beyond words. Those children that Ed Romero told us about, they and their parents were victims. If I did what Ed says I did, if I changed the appearance of children, it was no different than what I'm doing now in the courtroom. Someone has to look out for the victims."

Brad pulled Juanita close.

"I'm ready to go home. I'm ready to get back to work. There are Luther Birdwells to prosecute. There are always children who need their hair dyed. There are so many victims. So many victims." Juanita became quiet. "There are so many Luther Birdwells."

Another satellite arced across the night sky.

"Let's go home, Brad. Let's go home."

Pulling Juanita into an embrace, Brad held the love of his life.

"Wait one second, Juanita. I have something for us. I have something we need to hear right now." Rising from the steps, Brad entered their room. Within seconds, he was back with his cell phone. Once again tucked beneath the blanket, his fingers flicked over the screen. He found what he wanted. "This is a song that I've heard a million times. A piece of music that was written for us, Juanita, it was written for us. Let me hold you close. Listen."

*It was no accident me finding you*
  *Someone had a hand in it*
  *Long before we ever knew*

The voice of Tracy Byrd softly carried through the night.

*Now I just can't believe you're in my life*
  *Heaven's smiling down on me*
  *As I look at you tonight*

Hair falling over Juanita's shoulders.
Brad's touch.
Breathing as one.
Hearts beating.

*I tip my hat to the keeper of the stars*

*He sure knew what he was doing*
*When he joined these two hearts*

*It was no accident me finding you*
*Someone had a hand in it*
*Long before we ever knew*

*Thanks to the keeper of the stars*

Music faded but their embrace held. "That was beautiful, Brad. Thank you."

"I can't explain things either, Juanita. But yes, you are correct. God, or someone out there," Brad now swept his hand across the sky, "has a purpose for you. And that same God or spirit had a hand in bringing you and me together. The Keeper of the Stars, Juanita, the Keeper of the Stars. Someone had a hand in it, long before we ever knew."

A rush of air disturbed the night. Fluttering. Coming to rest on the stair railing, mere feet from Juanita and Brad, the owl's hoot was soft as starlight.

# GRATITUDE

*A Candle in a Cathedral* would never have happened without the support of my wife. I am a blessed man to share life with such an incredible woman.

# AUTHOR'S NOTE

*A Candle in a Cathedral* is a work of fiction. The Taos Revolt of 1847 is a fact of history. Based upon the testimony of witnesses and survivors, historians have compiled thousands of words to preserve this slice of our nation's development.

The tragedy of children being killed if "gringo" blood was suspected to be in their veins is a documented aspect of the Taos Revolt. The stories of efforts by parents to dye hair or alter the appearance of children have been documented from witnesses and survivors.

To the best of my knowledge, there is not a grave in the Kit Carson Cemetery holding the bodies of persons named Manuel Lujan or Juanita Lujan. The Taos Public Library maintains a ledger of all persons known to be buried in the cemetery. According to these records, no such grave exists.

The Millicent Rogers Museum is a jewel. The history and art of Taos and of the Southwest are displayed in an atmosphere of elegance and reverence. The letter written by Millicent Rogers is powerful. Her words speak not only to her son, but to generations of famous and ordinary people who are the history of the Southwest and the Enchanted Land of New Mexico.

# ABOUT THE AUTHOR

Dale spent twenty-five years as an FBI agent investigating violent crimes and concluded his law enforcement career by helping establish the Federal Air Marshal Service. He then turned his energy to writing. Dale lives in Colorado where fly fishing, mountains and the grandeur of nature have been integral to him, his wife, and their three children.